Fate was one of those things like ghosts. I didn't believe in them, but I didn't not believe in them. I didn't have enough evidence to make an informed choice either way. So I stayed neutral. Nonetheless, I had a healthy respect for both ghosts and fate. Enough that I tried to stay out of their way.

I heard piano music before I even pushed the saloon door open. Saloon. Hotel. Maggie insisted that I would like it. Apparently, since there was no way she could know that firsthand, she had learned it from one of my siblings. Right now I wasn't too happy with my siblings, especially the one who had gotten me here, but all in all, I trusted their decisions.

A young lady dressed in an old west costume—a low-cut red ruffled dress and hair piled on top of her head, played the grand piano on one side of the room. The dining tables were all taken. And unlike the girl playing the piano, the people at the tables looked like regular, modern tourists and maybe some locals here and there.

The bartender standing behind the counter with the standard mirror behind him, making the bottles of alcohol look twice as abundant, was dressed in old-west fashion as well. And… it seemed like he must be the one I needed to talk to about my room since I didn't see any other place to check in.

"You have a reservation?" the bartender asked. His name tag identified him as Wyatt.

"Yes." I rested my tote bag on the nearest empty barstool. "Isabella Fleming."

Wyatt produced a key. "Been expecting you," he said. "One of the Flemings."

"Yes," I said, taking the oversized silver key from his hand. "Try not to hold it against me."

Wyatt laughed. "Don't worry. We're Fleming friendly around Whiskey Springs."

"Good to know," I said, shouldering my tote bag and turning around to look for the best pathway to the stairs. "I'm just here for the night." I glanced back at him over my shoulder.

Wyatt nodded, keeping his expression neutral. "Good luck with that," he said.

"Thanks," I said and kept walking. My brother was going to pay for this one. He owed me big time.

All I wanted to do was get up tomorrow, get to Denver, and board my airplane back to Houston. In the meantime, I would stay in my room.

If I stayed in my room, surely I could avoid whatever marriage fever had infected my siblings.

AN OLD FASHIONED CHRISTMAS

ALSO BY KATHRYN KALEIGH

Contemporary Romance
The Worthington Family

The Heart of Christmas

The Magic of Christmas

In a One Horse Open Sleigh

A Secret Royal Christmas

An Old-Fashioned Christmas

Second Chance Kisses

Second Chance Secrets

First Time Charm

Three Broken Rules

Second Chance Destiny

Unexpected Vows

Billionaire's Unexpected Landing

Billionaire's Accidental Girlfriend

Billionaire Fallen Angel

Begin Again

Love Again

Falling Again

Just Stay

Just Chance

Just Believe

Just Us

Just Once

Just Happened

Just Maybe
Just Pretend
Just Because

AN OLD FASHIONED CHRISTMAS

THE WORTHINGTONS

KATHRYN KALEIGH

To learn more about Kathryn Kaleigh, visit

www.kathrynkaleigh.com

Kathryn Kaleigh

1

ISABELLA FLEMING

*B*oys. Did they all have to be such idiots?

Especially my brothers. They were the worst.

And I happened to have the misfortune of having three of them, all older.

It was a beautiful day for flying. With the deep roar of the engine surrounding me, I could fall into an almost meditative state, allowing my thoughts to wander where they would.

I leveled the airplane off at ten thousand feet. My favorite height for flying. From this elevation I could see rivers and patches of green fields and forests. Towns, all connected by highways. Sometimes I found myself following the roads with my eyes. Imagining what it would be like to be down there. Driving a car. It wasn't that I didn't drive. I had a sweet little BMW that I drove all around Houston. But still... I couldn't help but wonder.

Where would I be going?

The pale blue sky stretched out in front of me, the morning sun reflecting off wisps of white clouds blending with the hazy edge of the earth at the horizon.

It was four days before Christmas and I had to clean up my brother Greyson's mess.

I had no complaints about flying. It was what I was born to do. They said I had my Grandpa Noah's genes. The highest of all compliments.

If there was ever a better man born, I would have to meet him to believe it.

Houston born and bred, I'd lived there all my life. As a pilot, I had made hundreds of stops at cities, small towns, even airports in the middle of nowhere. But I had never taken a road trip. Not once. Not even in college. Our idea of a road trip back then was grabbing a classmate, hopping into a Cessna, and flying someplace for a lunch or even a dinner.

My gaze swept automatically over the gauges and monitors. This Phenom lived in the little town of Whiskey Springs, Colorado, deep in the mountains just west of Denver. But my brother, also a pilot, and his new bride had left it in Houston when they boarded a commercial flight to someplace in Eastern Canada.

So now I had to get the plane to Whiskey Springs so my other brother, also a pilot, could put it back into commission. This airplane was currently the only Skye Travels airplane housed in Whiskey Springs by my grandfather's private airline company.

Grandpa Noah Worthington had taken a single little Cessna airplane and used it to establish the foundation of a successful company. One that rivaled the big airlines.

When newly licensed pilots went searching for jobs, the most coveted was working for Skye Travels owned and run by Noah Worthington. And his children and their children. Skye Travels was family owned and family run along with dozens of other pilots, some even living in other parts of the country. It was a modern world, after all. But Houston was the hub of it all.

After leaning over to grab a bottle of water, I adjusted the four-point harness across my shoulders and waist.

The Phenom's stunningly beautiful piano black interior still smelled like new.

It was only the second time I had flown it.

And even though all three of my brothers lived in Whiskey Springs, this was the first time I had been to the little town.

All I had to do was to drop the airplane off, then get an Uber into Denver where I would catch a commercial flight back to Houston.

That was all.

I blew out a sigh. I was going to have a busy day.

As I caught a glimpse of the Dallas metropolis airport on radar, it occurred to me that I didn't have a plane ticket back home. I couldn't even remember the last time I'd flown commercial.

I needed to call the Skye Travels front desk to see if Maggie had taken care of that. Fortunately, the Phenom had Wifi.

WESLEY BENNETT

*L*ively piano music drifted from the first floor of the saloon, but it was quiet enough in my room. Quiet enough that I could hear the steady ticking of the round wooden clock across from the bed. There was no standard electric digital clock on the nightstand—just a phone charger. The room was an interesting merger of modern and old.

My room, at the end of the hall, held one queen sized four-poster bed, an antique mahogany dresser with drawers and a hanging rod. A small bathroom. No closet.

The saloon had been built in the 1800s. The first building in fact, built in Whiskey Springs. The slogan at the time had something to do with a never-ending flow of whiskey. And according to all accounts, they still had a steady supply of the famous whiskey. Interestingly enough, this had been both a saloon and a hotel back then, too. Some people lived in these rooms for various reasons such as while building their permanent homes.

If I stared out the window at the tall rugged mountain peaks in the distance and ignored the modern plumbing and electric, I could easily imagine myself back there in the 1800s.

A magnificent eagle flew across the valley, landing in one of the thousands of spruce, pine, and fir trees. There were a few aspen trees, too. The perfect elevation, as far as I was concerned.

I ran a hand down the window casing. This could very well be an original window frame. The glass with its imperfect waves was most definitely original.

The downstairs saloon level was interesting, too. A girl wearing a saloon-girl dress played the piano like there was no tomorrow. It was crowded, too. I'd been going to grab some lunch, but there were no empty tables.

I didn't mind, really. I could put in an hour's worth of work, then go back down and surely, by then, there would be an empty table or maybe even an unoccupied barstool.

It was four days until Christmas and outside of the typical tourist season, this was the busiest time of year for Whiskey Springs.

There was actually a Christmas tree in my room. A full six foot fully decorated Christmas tree. Everything in Whiskey Springs that didn't move got draped with twinkling lights or garland or some kind of festive decoration.

If my room was on the other side of the hotel I would be able to look down at Main Street and would no doubt be able to hear the strains of Christmas music piped through speakers along the sidewalk.

If Christmas was a town, it would be Whiskey Springs.

I was supposed to have flown out today, but the private jet I was supposed to fly out on hadn't arrived yet. Delayed in Houston.

I'd used the time to learn about the history of the town and soak in the ambiance. Ambiance that was currently Christmas trees and festive music and twinkling lights.

It was supposed to snow tomorrow, but I would be out of here by then. On my way to Pittsburgh... and Christmas... with family.

Since the airplane was delayed, maybe my luck would hold and it would snow enough tonight to keep me here a few days. Until after Christmas would be perfect. Didn't seem like too terribly much to ask.

Wishful thinking, I told myself, as I turned away from the window.

I poured myself a glass of whiskey, mostly just because it was there, and studied the amber liquid as it swirled in the glass.

I sat in the armchair across from the bed and enjoyed having some time to just sit and think. It was so rare to have that.

The sparkling light from the chandelier overhead and the clear twinkling lights on the tree chased away any gloominess that might try to seep into the room.

This saloon... hotel... had a positive feel to it.

Might be the lights. Might be the lively music drifting from downstairs.

As one song ended, I imagined the girls changing out and another one sitting down to play. This one didn't play quite as good as the one before, but if enthusiasm counted, she was holding her own.

I swirled the liquid some more, then took a sip. The whiskey burned all the way down my throat. I coughed. Glad I didn't embarrass myself by trying to drink some of this downstairs. It was bad enough embarrassing myself in private.

My stomach growled, reminding me that I'd come upstairs to work while some of the lunch crowd cleared out. The bartender had offered to send up room service, but I hadn't seen the need for that.

There was a fine line between isolating and needing a few minutes to just sit and think.

I opened the lid of my computer, used my fingerprint to unlock it, then stared at the blinking cursor.

Wasn't much point in trying to work now. If I got lost in my work, I'd miss lunch altogether. I closed the lid and shoved the computer aside. I was a firm believer in working hard. But I also knew, from experience, that a break was needed now and then.

Balance. That was the key. Balance between work and play. Both were absolutely necessary to a healthy human condition.

The atmosphere here at the Whiskey Springs hotel—at Christmastime—made it difficult to focus on work.

I slid over a flyer with the Christmas activity schedule I had picked up downstairs.

Tomorrow night there was a Christmas tree decorating contest in the high school gym. The trees would then be donated to charity.

The next night there was some kind of narrow-gauge train ride. Sounded like something for kids. Then the next night—on Christmas Eve—there was a Christmas party for the adults, but according to the flyer, it was family friendly.

Whiskey Springs was a family-friendly kind of town.

I had no family of my own. I almost had, but things had gone sideways. Looking back, it was for the best. Bailey Monroe was not the kind of girl a man like me would do well settling down with.

She was model-beautiful and loved everything related to fashion, but it had been difficult to hold a conversation with her for more than a few minutes. She had a strange way of looking at the world. One that I never quite got the hang of.

But then I was the science guy. And even though they say opposites attract, the truth was that birds of a feather flock together.

So Bailey had flocked her way on over to a guy she'd dated in high school. They had reconnected on social media. Go figure. I'd wished her a happy life and happily gone about my way. It was funny, really. I often didn't have a good sense of how I felt about a girl until after she was gone.

Instead of being upset about Bailey, I'd actually felt a sense of relief. That told me that I had dodged a bullet, so to speak.

Going over to the sink, I splashed cold water on my face. And I would actually call it ice cold, if I wanted to be precise.

Since I wasn't getting anything done up here, I grabbed my phone off the charger and made my way back downstairs. If there wasn't a table open yet, I would just wait.

3

ISABELLA

*T*here was always more turbulence flying near the mountains. I suppose a pilot would get used to it, but being from Texas and serving that general southern area, the severity of the turbulence near the mountains always caught me off-guard. Today was no different.

Other than those couple of pockets of unexpected turbulence, my flight into Whiskey Springs was uneventful.

Grandpa Noah had taught me when I was knee-high to a tadpole that an uneventful flight was the only kind of flight that would let a pilot get old. Any other kind, especially the kind that involved a careless pilot would not end well.

I took the Phenom in for a smooth landing. I was good at landings. Probably my favorite part of flying. I'd practiced taking off and landing so many times that I could do it in my sleep. Not that I would. I still got that surge of adrenalin when I stepped into a cockpit. The kind that made it hard to believe that I was going to be the one to take this plane into the air and bring it safely back down again.

I stood on Main Street directly in front of the Whiskey

Springs Saloon. Maggie, the person who had been running Skye Travels as long as I could remember, had made a reservation for me here. Said it was the only place in town that had a room available for tonight.

Sparkly Christmas lights twinkled up and down the street. And Christmas music blasted out of speakers up and down the street.

It was cold, cold enough for my heavy coat and cold enough that I wished I had gloves and a scarf, but not snowing. It seemed like it should be snowing.

I hoisted my overnight bag over my shoulder. I had everything I needed for an overnight stay. Hadn't used the bag in a long time. It was supposed to be for unplanned stay-overs. I always packed a real suitcase for planned trips.

This was about as unplanned as they came, I guess. I was supposed to just drop off the airplane. What was it about Whiskey Springs? The little town had captured the attention of all three of my brothers AND my older sister. They had all four found their soulmates here. At least that's what they all claimed.

This was just a little town in the mountains. How was it even possible that all four of my siblings had found true love here? And, to be quite honest, I was feeling a little nervous about being here.

I wasn't dating anyone right now and the thought of fate bringing me here to meet someone just quite frankly scared me more than I could even think about.

I hadn't even decided whether I wanted to get married or not.

Fate was one of those things like ghosts. I didn't believe in them, but I didn't not believe in them. I didn't have enough evidence to make an informed choice either way. So I stayed neutral. Nonetheless, I had a healthy respect for both ghosts and fate. Enough that I tried to stay out of their way.

I heard piano music before I even pushed the saloon door open. Saloon. Hotel. Maggie insisted that I would like it. Apparently, since there was no way she could know that firsthand, she had learned it from one of my siblings. Right now I wasn't too happy with my siblings, especially the one who had gotten me here, but all in all, I trusted their decisions.

A young lady dressed in an old west costume—a low-cut red ruffled dress and hair piled on top of her head, played the grand piano on one side of the room. The dining tables were all taken. And unlike the girl playing the piano, the people at the tables looked like regular, modern tourists and maybe some locals here and there.

The bartender standing behind the counter with the standard mirror behind him, making the bottles of alcohol look twice as abundant, was dressed in old-west fashion as well. And… it seemed like he must be the one I needed to talk to about my room since I didn't see any other place to check in.

"You have a reservation?" the bartender asked. His name tag identified him as Wyatt.

"Yes." I rested my tote bag on the nearest empty barstool. "Isabella Fleming."

Wyatt produced a key. "Been expecting you," he said. "One of the Flemings."

"Yes," I said, taking the oversized silver key from his hand. "Try not to hold it against me."

Wyatt laughed. "Don't worry. We're Fleming friendly around Whiskey Springs."

"Good to know," I said, shouldering my tote bag and turning around to look for the best pathway to the stairs. "I'm just here for the night." I glanced back at him over my shoulder.

Wyatt nodded, keeping his expression neutral. "Good luck with that," he said.

"Thanks," I said and kept walking. My brother was going to pay for this one. He owed me big time.

All I wanted to do was get up tomorrow, get to Denver, and board my airplane back to Houston. In the meantime, I would stay in my room.

If I stayed in my room, surely I could avoid whatever marriage fever had infected my siblings.

4

BENNETT

I had ended up spending most of my day walking about town. Managed to snag a few western themed trinkets for my family. A coffee mug with a grizzly bear on it. A t-shirt with *Whiskey Springs* splashed across the front. A coffee table book of paintings by one of the early founders, a woman by the last name of Auclair.

I'd sort them all out when I got to Pittsburg. Figure out who got what. I'd already bought some gift cards to wrap up, so everyone would get something they liked.

By the time the sun dropped below the rugged mountain peaks, I was freshly showered and dressed to go downstairs. I hadn't gotten any work done all day, but I wasn't concerned. I would make it up later.

Right now, I was thinking about some fried food and a whiskey.

Just before I headed out, my phone chimed with a text message. Scowling at Bailey's name on my screen, I almost ignored it. But curiosity got the best of me. Even though she had burned her bridges with me, it wasn't in my nature to ignore someone I'd cared about, even if we had broken up.

BAILEY: *Just wanted to check in. Make sure you made it to Pittsburgh.*

I did not want to start a conversation with Bailey. She was in my past. But I answered her anyway. I was, after all, a gentleman.

ME: *Still traveling. Have a good holiday.*

Then I turned off the volume and slipped my phone in my jacket pocket.

I just wanted to have a quiet evening to myself. I'd go downstairs, have a burger and fries. A whiskey. And come back up for an early night. The last notice I'd gotten from Skye Travels was that the plane had actually arrived and would be ready to leave at my convenience.

They apologized profusely for the delay and offered me a substantial discount on my next flight. I wasn't sure whether to be impressed or wary. A little of both, actually. An apology with a marketing ploy.

Skye Travels had a stellar reputation, so I knew I was reading too much into it. They were apologizing for the flight not being here as promised.

Maybe I was actually a little disappointed since I'd sort of hoped I'd get another day out of the delay.

So tomorrow I would be in Pittsburgh with my family.

That meant that I had tonight before being hit with twenty questions by my family.

What happened between you and Bailey?

Are you seeing anyone else?

Does this mean you can stay longer?

Having two younger sisters was sometimes a bit of a pain. It didn't help that my mother was exactly the same way. They wanted to know everything, even when they didn't need to.

I locked my door and headed downstairs to the saloon part of the building.

The piano was still playing. I wondered just how many girls they had rotating at the piano through the day. I could only imagine that it could only be a managerial nightmare.

The saloon was a bit more crowded than it had been at lunch. At bit louder. A bit less family oriented.

There were a lot of couples and a lot of groups. Probably people either visiting here or coming here as a family for the holidays.

Whiskey Springs was, after all, a destination town. Summer and Christmas were their busy times.

I could definitely see the attraction. Magnificent eagles flying across the valley. Rugged snow-capped mountain peaks. And if a person loved Christmas, this was most definitely the place to be. Christmas had opened up and spilled all over the little town. And it wasn't just the decorations and the music, it was the feeling. The festive atmosphere.

I'd heard several people remark about how unusual it was that it wasn't snowing. It, apparently, had been a long time since they'd had a Christmas without snow.

The mountains were snow-capped and it was icy cold. A person couldn't stay outside very long without some type of head covering. I'd made that mistake and had gotten an ear ache out of it. Fortunately the ear ache had cleared up when I went inside one of the stores and bought myself a scarf. A bright red scarf.

Even though I wasn't planning to go outside, I draped it around my neck anyway as I stood looking around for a place to sit.

The place was noisy and crowded. I didn't even try to snag a table. I found a bar stool at one end of the bar between an older burly man and a younger man, both drinking beer from bottles. Neither of them paid me much attention. They were watching a football game on the television.

I, on the other hand, ordered myself a whiskey.

When a man was in Whiskey Springs, a man had to drink whiskey. It was a thing.

ISABELLA

*I*t turned out not to be so difficult to spend the afternoon in my room.

It wasn't a bad room. A combination of modern and old. The four-poster queen bed was draped with gauzy white curtains tied at each of the four corners. The room actually had a live blue spruce Christmas tree draped with twinkling clear lights and tasteful white and blue ribbons and balls.

It was a really nice touch. I intermittently stared at it and paced my room as I talked to my mother. Two of my aunts. And even Grandpa Noah.

I was looking forward to Christmas Eve. The one night the whole extended Worthington family came together.

The last couple of years, however, one or more of my siblings had been absent. They were spending time with their husband's or their wife's families.

It was what happened as we began to marry and have families of our own.

I was not ready for that. Not for myself. I had plenty of guy friends and I knew how they operated. Granted they were all pilots and pilots did not have the best of reputations.

Unfortunately I had seen my share of substantiating evidence for that bad reputation.

So I kept myself busy with work. Maybe later.

As I watched the sunset from my window I got a sense of what drew people here. I didn't know much about the little town, but the view couldn't be beat.

I lived in an apartment on the fifteenth floor of a high rise, so I'd seen my share of sunsets and sunrises, too, for that matter. But the way the light faded as the sun dropped over the tall mountain peaks was absolutely stunning.

After the sun went down and there was nothing else to see outside the window, I paced my room a bit. I would have changed clothes, but, of course, I only had one change and I had to wear that tomorrow. So I was stuck wearing my dark gray skirt and white button-down shirt. Basic pilot's uniform.

I tried calling my sister, but it went straight to voicemail.

I checked my email. Confirmed my flight scheduled to leave Denver in the morning. Checked out the Uber app and scheduled a car.

It wasn't like I didn't have things to do.

It was nearly seven o'clock when I realized I hadn't eaten anything all day. At least not that I could remember.

And now that I'd thought about food, I couldn't stop thinking about it.

I called downstairs to ask about room service. They said they were too busy to take room service orders, but I was welcome to come down and eat.

I hung up and stared at the phone. How could that possibly make a difference? If they were too busy to bring me room service, wouldn't they be just as busy downstairs serving me at a table?

I had no way to answer that question, so I unclipped my hair, ran a hairbrush through it, and decided to leave it down.

I slipped back into my shoes, grabbed my crossbody

handbag, and steeled myself for going downstairs. Surely I could have dinner without getting engaged.

Just because my siblings had found the people they wanted to marry here, did not mean that I would. In fact, since I knew about the risk, I felt protected. Or so I told myself.

Inoculated, I decided as I turned the doorknob. Knowledge and forewarning equaled inoculation.

BENNETT

*B*y eight o'clock the restaurant had, by my estimation, turned into an actual saloon befitting its name.

It was crowded and loud. Someone had turned up the television and a college football game was in full swing.

The local favorite team was winning if the cheers coming from the guys drinking beer and whiskey at the bar was any indication.

There were still a few tables occupied by people not interested in football, being entertained by the piano music. It created an interested, but not necessarily discordant background.

Every now and then someone came in or out, letting in a burst of cold air. According to the conversation swirling around me, there was still no snow and it didn't seem to be in the forecast. The occasional news announcement on the television corroborated the local opinion about this being an accurate state of the weather in the area. It wasn't just Whiskey Springs that was bereft of a white Christmas.

Boulder. Fort Collins. Denver. None of the towns and cities in the valley were forecasted to have a white Christmas. Most people were disappointed. A few grinches were happy there was no snow to drive in or to shovel.

Personally, I was rooting for snow. A freak snowstorm would be just great right about now. And us pro-snow people outnumbered the no-snow people at least three to one.

That should stand for something.

My phone vibrated in my pocket. It was my mother.

"Hello."

"Hi Mom." I held my hand over the phone, trying to block the loud bar sounds, but of course she heard the noise anyway.

"Sounds like you're busy," she said.

"Just grabbing some dinner," I said.

"At ten o'clock at night." It wasn't a question. Just a statement. Mom did not tend to be judgmental, but like all good mothers, she worried.

"Mom," I said. "It's eight o'clock over here."

"Right." She hesitated and I could hear the frustration in her voice.

"Hold on," I said, swirling around on the bar stool and sliding off.

I stepped out into the cold air. There was still music coming through the sidewalk speakers, but it was most definitely quieter than it was inside the saloon.

"Is your flight still scheduled for tomorrow?" she asked.

"As far as I know." Someone stepped outside the saloon letting the football game spill out. I walked a few more steps away from the door, my hand still over my ears. Mostly to keep the cold out now.

"I hope so," Mom said. "The sooner the better."

"Why's that?" I asked, a little spurt of alarm skittering up my spine.

"Well," Mom said. "The weather is supposed to start getting bad in the morning. Maybe tonight."

There was a God.

"How bad?" I asked.

"Blizzard," they said. "I don't really know for sure. You know how it is with the weather."

"I'm not sure what time I'll get out of here," I said. "But I'm sure the pilot will check the weather over there in the morning." And with any luck the flight plan would get rejected.

I read somewhere that there were only four possible answers to a prayer. Yes. No. Not now. And I have something else entirely planned for you.

Maybe this was a round about way of getting a yes to my wish to avoid Pittsburgh. And maybe... just maybe... staying in Whiskey Springs was part of the something else entirely.

ISABELLA

*a*s I walked down the stairs into the saloon restaurant, I had a better sense of why there was no one available to deliver room service.

I saw six different workers and they were all dashing here and there with obvious purpose. It looked like controlled chaos.

A quick glance told me there were no empty tables. I was okay with that. I had three older brothers and I worked in a male dominated world. I was okay with sitting at the bar.

Besides, I preferred the comfort of the football game on the television to the old-fashioned piano music. Just a personal preference.

I found an empty bar stool on the far end and hopped up onto the seat. Since I was the only female sitting at the bar, I expected a few curious glances from the men. I just ignored them as I ordered a glass of the house chardonnay.

The bad thing about this trip was that I didn't get to pilot myself home. And the one good thing about this trip was that I didn't have to pilot myself home. So chardonnay it was.

As I waited for the bartender to bring my glass of wine, I

watched the football game on the television. The Broncos scored a touchdown on the kickoff starting the third quarter.

I set my cell on the bar in front of me and answered the text from my sister.

MAKENNA: *Are you still in Whiskey Springs?*

ME: *Afraid so. Thanks to Greyson.*

The bartender set the glass of wine in front of me.

MAKENNA: *Say hello to Wyatt for me.*

I just stared at the screen.

"Can I get you anything else?" the bartender asked.

I looked up, blinking and my gaze landed on his nametag. *Wyatt.*

"Wyatt?" I asked, looking from him to my cell and back up again.

"Yes ma'am."

"Makenna says hi."

Wyatt grinned. "How's she doing?"

"Good. I think."

"Tell her I said hello."

"Okay," I said with a little nod and watched as Wyatt moved along to take someone else's order.

ME: *Hello back.*

MAKENNA: *Heard you'll be back tomorrow.*

ME: *I hope so. That's the plan anyway.*

MAKENNA: *The weather is unseasonably warm there this year.*

I swirled the wine in my glass and shivered as I thought about the icy cold wind sweeping from the snowcapped mountains. Warm obviously was subjective.

I lost myself deep in the conversation with Makenna as the noise of the television and the people around me swirled in the background.

The guy sitting next to me got up and left and a few minutes later, another sat down. I registered all this at an unconscious level.

"You're not from here," the new guy said.

I probably wouldn't even have noticed him except that he was leaning close, his face next to my shoulder.

Keeping my gaze straight ahead, I turned my phone over face down and took a sip of my wine. It wasn't bad for a place known for their whiskey.

I stalled, waiting for the guy to back off and leave me alone.

"Are you?" he persisted.

"No," I said, keeping my gaze straight ahead, focusing on the liquor bottles on the shelf beneath the huge gilded mirror.

"You alone?" he asked. I smelled the whiskey on his breath and prided myself on not recoiling.

"Working," I said, turning my phone back over and tapping the screen. Not wanting him to see my messages with my sister, I opened my weather app and stalled some more, hoping he would get the idea and leave me alone.

"A little late for work," he said.

I looked up, hoping to catch the attention of the bartender, but he was otherwise occupied at the other end of the bar. Something happened in the football game. Something that had the men yelling at the screen.

So I was basically alone in a sea of people with the guy next to me.

"Gotta go," I said, twirling on the stool.

The man put a hand on my arm. "You're from the south," he said. "I love me some southern girls."

The man was in his thirties. Rather nondescript. A little scruffy. Even if I was interested in a diversion, which I wasn't, he was not my type.

I didn't even necessarily have a type, but whatever it was, he was not it.

I glanced down meaningfully at his hand on my arm, then back up to his eyes. He was either too stupid or too drunk to see the warning in my glance. Or maybe he just didn't care.

"I said I'm going now."

"Aw now. The party's just starting honey. Don't leave now."

"Let go of me," I said, through clenched teeth.

"Just stay a little longer."

I slid off the barstool, hoping he would lose his grip, but it only tightened. A glance around told me that no one even noticed. Someone always noticed. I actually felt a bit of fear. And he had me a disadvantaged angle as far as protecting myself went.

"No," I said, with a quick tug. My arm slipped free and I took a step away with a relief that this had been easily resolved.

Then I felt his hand back on my arm, tighter now.

"The lady said no."

A man stood in front of me, facing my offender.

"Nobody asked you," the jerk said.

"She said no."

Then all hell broke loose.

My protector slammed a fist into the jerk's face causing the jerk to release my arm, sending me backwards a couple of steps.

My rescuer managed to catch me without ever even taking his eyes off the jerk, who was now groaning and holding his nose.

"You broke my nose," he said.

"You so much as look in this lady's general direction again and I'll break your whole face."

The jerk grumbled something under his breath.

My protector grabbed the jerk by the collar of his shirt and pulled him off the bar stool until their faces were only inches apart.

"I won't tell you again," he said. "Do you understand?"

The jerk nodded. My protector pushed the jerk backward. Crashing into the bar stools, he fell against two other men before he hit the floor.

And, of course, now, everyone was looking our direction.

There was a commotion as the men helped the jerk up, then escorted him out the door.

Only then did I look at the guy who had come to my rescue.

"Thank you," I said, looking into deep sparkling blue eyes in a ruggedly handsome face.

"You're welcome," he said and I realized his hand was still on my arm, keeping me steady. But I didn't mind.

"I had it under control," I said, straightening my jacket.

"I noticed." He was smiling a lopsided grin at me. "I've just snagged a table over there if you'd like to sit with me."

"I 'um… I had a glass of wine." But the space where I had been sitting had been closed up by the men, more intent on watching the game than worrying about someone punching a jerk in the nose.

"I'll order you another one," he said.

I nodded with a glance toward the door.

"He won't be back."

"How do you know?" I asked, hesitating.

"Because he knows that if he comes back in here, he'll have more than a bloody nose."

Then, realizing he was headed to his table, I hurried to catch up.

He held my chair while I sat, then he sat across from me.

"I'm Wesley," he said.

Wesley. My knight-in-shining armor was Wesley.

A server appeared at our side. The server was a tall, lean clean-cut young man, probably a college student. He had a pleasant and discreet manner about him.

"Would you get the lady a fresh glass of whatever she was drinking and a whiskey for me?"

Surely it wouldn't hurt to sit here. Just for a few minutes while I settled myself.

8

WESLEY

*M*y intent tonight had not been to rescue a damsel in distress.

After standing outside talking to my mother, freezing my ears off, I went back inside and instantly snagged a table.

The men watching the football game were louder than they had been earlier. And the louder they got, the louder the television got or so it seemed.

The server, a friendly young college aged fellow brought me a menu and I settled back to study it, even though I already knew I just wanted a burger and fries. Good thing I looked. They had seven different variations.

After quickly choosing a burger, I sat back and took a sip of water.

It only took a split second for my gaze to land on the alluring brunette sitting on a barstool. Sitting in the midst of a crowd of men, she was looking down, focused on her phone, ignoring the shouts and cheers, ignoring everything actually about the men.

Her gently wavy hair falling halfway down her back was shorter around her face, slanting to a longer length in the back.

She was wearing black pants and a matching suit jacket with an untucked white oxford shirt beneath.

I could only see her profile, but even from here I watched her red bow shaped lips curve into a smile as she tapped a message on her phone.

How was it she sat unnoticed in a sea of men?

Then it happened. One man, sitting closest to her, left and another slid into his place. But this new one noticed her.

He spoke to her, but she ignored him. I couldn't hear what he was saying, but she kept her gaze straight ahead. His attentions were obviously unwanted.

Just as the football fans started yelling at the television, the man put a hand on her arm.

Oh no. This was not going to do.

I was up from my chair in a flash, going on pure instinct.

But before I could get to them, she had slid off her barstool, no doubt thinking she would easily walk away. But I knew better. I saw the way the man was looking at her.

By the time he grabbed her arm a second time, I was there.

"The lady said no." I barely recognized my own voice.

I stood between them, as much as I could, considering that he had a hand on her arm.

"Nobody asked you."

"She said no."

The man sneered. He actually sneered at me.

There was no way he was going to walk out of here with this woman. I didn't care if they were married. I hauled back and slammed my fist into his face.

As he released his grip on the girl, I balanced her to keep her from falling back.

The jerk groaned and held his bloody nose. I didn't look away from him.

"You broke my nose," he said.

I leaned forward. "Damn right," I said for his ears only.

Then louder. "You so much as look in this lady's general direction again and I'll break your whole face."

The jerk grumbled something under his breath.

I grabbed the man by the collar of his shirt and jerked him off the bar stool.

"I won't tell you again," I said. "Do you understand?"

He nodded.

But there was something in his eyes didn't sit right with me.

I shoved him backwards. He crashed into the bar stools behind him, and slammed into two other men before he hit the floor.

The man was hauled out in short order by some of the other men.

I waited to see if there were going to be any ramifications for me. The men must have been paying more attention to what had happened than I gave them credit for. Like nothing happened, they got back to their football game.

I turned to my damsel in distress and introduced myself.

"I'm Wesley," I said.

She just looked blankly from me to the door and back again. Since she couldn't just stand here, I urged her to sit with me at my table.

The girl straightened and seemed to collect herself by the time the server came and took our drink order.

Then her eyes locked onto mine and something shifted inside me.

It was a little bit like being socked in the gut. An undeniable attraction.

Her eyes were a deep emerald green framed by thick dark lashes.

She was young, somewhere in her mid-twenties, but her eyes held a depth that was almost unsettling.

"I'm Isabella," she said, her red lips curving into a little smile. "Thank you for the rescue, but I really can't stay."

9

ISABELLA

The server set a glass of chardonnay in front of me. After thanking him, I picked it up, swirled it, breathing in the rich scent, and took a big swallow.

Somehow the television kept getting louder and as it got louder, the men got louder. It was a close game. The kind of game that men enjoyed yelling at.

Even with the television and the men yelling at every play, good and bad, I could still hear the piano music. The two sounds did not mix. In my head, they sounded discordant. I preferred order. One thing at the time.

I set my glass down, then clasped my hands in my lap to keep them from trembling.

It had been disconcerting to feel alone in a sea of men. I was unsettled.

I glanced toward the door again, then back to Wesley.

As I gazed into his sparkling blue eyes with a hint of a smile, I studied him. He fit in here, I decided, but was not necessarily from here. That part I wasn't so good at figuring out.

He was studying me the same way I was studying him.

"Have you eaten?" he asked, ignoring my declaration that I couldn't stay.

"No," I shook my head. And unfortunately, I hadn't even gotten around to ordering anything yet, so I could claim to have anything to take with me to my room.

"They're too busy for room service and it's too cold to go outside," he said. "You might as well stay here and eat."

"You cover all the bases, huh?" He had effectively shot down all my excuses.

"I try." He was smiling at me again. Just a hint of a smile. Like he was secretly amused.

And there was a tough no-nonsenseness about him, as well. Part of that probably came from the way he had punched the jerk in the nose without even a moment's hesitation.

"Okay," I said. "I'll eat. But then I have to go back to my room."

"I don't blame you for wanting to stay away from all this." He made a little motion with his hand, indicating the noisy saloon restaurant.

"No," I said. "It's not..." I stopped. I didn't want to tell him the real reason I had to be cautious in Whiskey Springs.

Besides, there was no one in this room that I would consider marriage material. Wesley included.

I took a deep breath and smiled at him. "Thank you," I said. "For busting that guy's nose and for sharing your table."

Before he could respond, the server came back to take our orders. I didn't have a menu, so I didn't have anything in mind.

"What would you like?" Wesley asked.

"I'll have whatever you're having," I said, running a finger along the stem of my wine glass. I didn't feel like going through the trouble of looking at a menu.

"Two old-fashioned burgers and fries," Wesley said.

I smiled again as the waiter walked away.

"What's funny?" he asked.

"Not funny," I said. "Just… unexpected."

"Please don't tell me you're a vegetarian."

"No," I said. "I'm not a vegetarian. I eat just about anything."

Now he grinned at me.

"I would have lost that bet."

"Why?" I asked, curiously.

"I had you pegged as someone who was very particular."

I glanced at the piano across the room. The old-fashioned costumed girl was playing Jingle Bells. "I am. About some things. About other things, not so much."

He held up his glass. "To being particular about things that matter."

I held up my glass, watching him with curiosity. I had to admit that I was not only impressed by Wesley, but I was also intrigued.

I looked away quickly, my smile vanishing.

This was not good. I could not risk any level of interest.

Fortunately, Wesley was not my type.

10

WESLEY

*E*ven though I assured Isabella that the jerk would not be returning, I watched the door every time it opened. I was pretty sure of my perceptions, but I also wouldn't risk being so cocky that I missed stupidity.

I considered it a win that Isabella had agreed to have dinner with me.

She was an intriguing combination of confidence—she had been boldly and blithely sitting alone in a group of rowdy men —and wariness. The wariness I understood.

The fact that she had been sitting in a group of men and no one had noticed what had been going on right beneath their noses was unsettling and she was smart to be wary.

"I guess I should have asked already," I said. "But do you know that man?"

"The jerk?"

"Yeah," I said hiding a smile that we had both named him *the jerk*.

"No," she said. "I've never been here before."

I nodded. "Would have gotten that one right."

"What gave me away?" she asked, seeming to relax a bit as we got into the conversation.

I leaned back in my chair, warming to the topic. "You're a city girl."

She tilted her head to the side. "You had a fifty-fifty chance on that one."

"You're right," I admitted. "I went for the easy one first."

"Got anything else?"

I glanced around. "You're the only one here wearing business clothes. And... there's something else before you rightly claim that one as easy, too."

"What else?"

"You aren't afraid of trying new foods."

She laughed. Just a little. But I was charmed. And I kept going.

"Not sure if you're wearing headphones or not, but you avoided talking to strangers."

She tucked a strand of hair behind an ear. "Who needs headphones when you have hair?"

I grinned.

"Okay," she said, leaning forward. "You are right. I am a city girl."

"Me too," I said. "A city guy."

"I would not have guessed that one," she said, taking a sip of her wine.

"Turn about is fair play. Why is that?"

"City guys don't punch guys in the nose at the bar. Not even to protect a lady's honor."

"Good point," I said, trying not to wince. "Can I tell you a secret?" I leaned forward. Lowered my voice.

She shrugged.

"I haven't done that since high school."

"I guess it's sort of like riding a bike."

"I guess it is."

The server brought our food and we ate in relative silence, considering everything going on around us.

She ate good. That surprised me. She was thin as a model, but she cleaned her plate.

I decided it would be impolite to mention that particular detail.

"Want anything else?" I asked. "I hear they have really good apple pie."

"No," she said. "But you go ahead."

"I'll pass." I drank the last of my whiskey and washed it down with the rest of my water.

She seemed to have forgotten that she couldn't stay.

And I found that I wanted her to stay. Very much.

"How about another drink?" I asked.

"I've met my quota for the night."

I wanted her to stay, but she wasn't making it easy.

11

ISABELLA

*T*he Broncos made another touchdown and the men at the bar erupted into a round of raucous cheering. This was an impressively spirited crowd. No doubt good for the saloon's business.

I rubbed my upper arm where the jerk had grabbed me. It was going to make a bruise. If I hadn't been so caught off guard, I could have socked him in the nose myself. I knew how to defend myself. I just hadn't had the occasion to use that particular knowledge.

Wesley was the kind of man a girl could feel safe with. I couldn't say what it was about him exactly.

He was a few years older than me. Probably early thirties. He had a strong jaw and a kind expression. It was his eyes, I decided. So deep and blue a girl could get lost in them.

Looking down, I realized my wine glass was empty.

I had no more excuses to stay. We'd had dinner. We'd finished our drinks.

And yet I wasn't compelled to leave.

It was because I was still shaky from the jerk grabbing my arm.

The saloon door opened and I looked over. But it was just a couple of guys heading out.

I was relieved that I was leaving here in the morning. Getting out of here. Otherwise I'd constantly be looking over my shoulder.

The jerk had just been drinking, I told myself. It wasn't even about me. He'd been drinking and I had been sitting there. Just one of those things that happened. Not personal.

But no matter what I told myself, it didn't stop me from feeling off-balance.

"How about another drink?" Wesley asked.

I looked back at him and was surprised by how just looking at him made my nerves settle.

I shook my head.

"I've met my quota for the night," I said.

Actually I'd gone over my quota. I rarely claimed the luxury of drinking. My grandfather's rule of twelve hours *bottle to throttle* had become so ingrained in my psyche that I didn't even risk it. A young, eager pilot, I took any flight I could get. And if I'd been drinking, well... a last minute flight would have to go to the next pilot on the list.

"My lips are kinda numb," I said, touching my lips. And my lipstick was long gone.

Wesley was grinning at me. "In that case, I'm definitely not leaving you alone."

"I think I need to go to the ladies' room," I said. Mostly I wanted to touch up my lipstick but I wasn't going to tell him that.

Wesley stood up and held out a hand. "I'll escort you," he said.

I put my hand in his and stood up. My legs felt a little weak and I was happy to have his hand for balance.

"I'm something of a lightweight," I said.

"I don't mind," he said, holding onto my hand. "It gives me an excuse to hold your hand."

I looked over at him sideways. He winked at me.

Feeling my skin heat, I turned away. I was not prone to blushing. What was it about this guy?

He released my hand when we reached the door to the ladies' room. "Don't be long," he said.

"I won't," I said with a glance over my shoulder. Wesley took his place on the wall just outside the restroom. Propped one foot on the wall behind him and prepared to wait.

I smiled to myself as I went into the restroom. It was like having my own private bodyguard. That and he would be waiting for me when I stepped out. That was an interesting sensation.

It was unusually quiet in the restroom, the music and noise from the television fading into the background.

I sat down in a chair in front of the mirror and surveyed my reflection. A quick swipe of red lipstick helped. I didn't wear a lot of makeup, but my mother had taught me to never leave home without red lipstick. Brianna Worthington Fleming had been a bold presence in the social media world of fashion. She had since moved on to other entrepreneurial projects, but at her core, she was all about fashion and beauty.

I took a deep breath and studied my reflection.

It was just one innocent night.

One night in Whiskey Springs with a stranger I was enjoying having a conversation with.

I would never see him again anyway. That particular thought sent a little inexplicable emotion along my spine that I couldn't quite interpret so I chose to ignore it.

It wasn't like I was going to have a one-night stand with him.

It was just conversation.

Tomorrow I was leaving. After tonight I'd never see him again. A little conversation couldn't hurt anything.

It didn't mean I had to marry him.

Assured that I had worked this whole thing out in my head, I opened the restroom door and stepped back out into the fray. Someone had turned the television down a notch and the men were much more subdued than when I had been out there just a few minutes earlier.

The smile on my lips faded and a scowl formed between my brows.

Wesley wasn't there.

12

WESLEY

*S*ometimes a man had to be careful what he wished for.

The answer to a prayer often came in unexpected ways. I was a firm believer that everything happened for a reason.

But tonight, my belief was a little shaky, to say the least.

Someone had turned down the television. That in itself worried me more than anything. Men like the ones at the bar did not seem prone to miss a single play without a very compelling reason.

I could see from the television screen that the game wasn't over and the men were still in their seats. Still sitting at the bar. It could be an intermission. Not halftime. It was past that. Then I realized, in a moment of utter perplexity that half a dozen of them were looking in my direction.

A man wearing a long black wool coat stood behind them, his back to me. I'd seen him come through the door. He was a middle-aged man, balding in the back, chewing gum. I'd dismissed him as a threat and returned my attention back to the ladies' room door.

It was only when he was standing three feet away from me, that I realized he was looking for me.

"Evening," he said.

I nodded, on alert now.

The television sound went back up, but the men had lost some of their enthusiasm.

"I'm not in line," I said, sweeping a hand to my right. "Men's room is open."

"Not here for the men's room." The man continued to chew his gum.

I straightened, pushing off the wall.

He reached into his pocket and pulled out a badge. Held it up.

"I'm Officer Stanley."

I remained calm on the outside, but on the inside, I groaned. I knew. I just knew. Trouble.

I looked back toward the door.

"Can I see your license?" he asked.

"Of course." I pulled out my money clip and slid out my driver's license, handing it over to him.

I knew better than to get into a bar fight.

It didn't matter that I had a good reason. It was against the law and I knew it.

"Seems you got yourself into a little trouble here earlier tonight."

"Wasn't much trouble," I said. "Just making sure a jerk learned not to put his hands on a lady."

"Uh huh," Officer Stanley said, one hand on his hip, still holding my license in his other hand. He hadn't so much as glanced at it.

"The jerk in question happens to be the police chief's son."

Well hell. "Then he should know not to force his attentions on a lady."

"Not your call," Officer Stanley said. "And certainly not your place to bloody his nose."

"It was done in the heat of the moment, Officer," I said. I didn't tell him about the way the jerk sneered at me. The way the man was looking at Isabella. The feeling in my gut that told me he was going to hound her relentlessly.

"Uh huh," he said again, sweeping a gaze behind him toward the bar where people were pretending not to watch.

"Look," I said. "I'll apologize for punching the guy in the nose. I might have gone a little overboard."

"I'm afraid that won't cut it," Officer Stanley said, chewing his gum. "We can do this here or we can go downtown."

"Do what?"

Officer Stanley opened his coat enough for me to catch a glimpse of handcuffs.

Hell. So that's how this was going.

"I'm waiting for—"

"Doesn't work like that." Officer Stanley said, his jaw working over the gum.

"Really," I said. "I'm more than willing to cooperate, but I just have—"

Officer Stanley took a step in my direction and looked into my eyes. He was close enough that I now knew that his gum had a minty flavor.

I held up my hands. I was losing this battle. Losing it fast. And it wasn't worth it. In the law's eyes, I was guilty. "Yes, sir."

With one last glance toward the ladies' room's closed door, I allowed myself to be peacefully escorted toward the front door.

My server met us there, my woolen coat draped over one arm.

"I'll come back," I said as I shrugged into my coat. "And take care of everything."

"Not to worry, Sir," he said.

I had nothing to do but worry, stepping outside into the

frigid air, walking to the police car, my entire life unraveling. A little dramatic perhaps, but riding, even in the front seat, down to the Whiskey Springs police station, was not how I had seen my evening going.

I had to fix this. I would fix it.

But what worried me the most was Isabella. Leaving her to think I had abandoned her.

And the worst part of all. I had no idea how to reach her. Not so much as a last name. If I had to stay in detention overnight, she could be gone when I got back.

The only thing I knew was that she lived in a city. Somewhere in the Texas region of the country.

As harsh as it was, I knew the reality.

I would never see her again.

13

ISABELLA

*a*fter finding Wesley gone from his post outside the restroom, not knowing what else to do, I walked back to our table.

Not only was his coat gone, but the table had been cleared.

I turned in a complete circle, but I didn't see him anywhere.

Everything else seemed normal. The men yelling at the television screen. The girl wearing the old-fashioned ruffled dress playing the piano. Servers rushing about. The same controlled chaos as before.

Maybe Wesley went to the restroom. Or maybe he stepped outside.

I decided I should just wait a few minutes. I pulled out the nearest chair and sat down on the edge of the seat.

I watched the door. The men at the bar. Everything.

Maybe he went up to his room. I shook my head. He said he would wait for me. I wasn't gone *that* long and he didn't seem like the kind of man who would go back on his word. He seemed like he *wanted* to wait for me.

"Ma'am?" It was our server, the affable young man. Right now, though, he looked more troubled than affable.

"Have you seen the man I was sitting with?" I asked.

The server glanced toward the bar, then sat in the chair next to mine.

Something was wrong. My heart rate tripped up with concern.

Had the jerk come back in? Had something happened to Wesley? All sorts of thoughts flashed through my head.

"Remember the man he punched at the bar?" he asked.

"Of course."

"That man is the police chief's son."

"And… that means?" I didn't know a lot about small towns, but I knew this particular news could not be good.

"Officer Stanley took Mr. Wesley downtown."

"Downtown? What does that mean?" I looked toward the door again.

"For questioning ma'am," the server said.

"Why couldn't he just question him here?" I had a really bad feeling about this. I'd watched just enough movies to have a general idea.

"It usually means an arrest," the server said.

My heart crashed against my chest, but I kept my voice low, almost a whisper. "Arrest? Why?"

"He assaulted a man."

"A man who assaulted me," I said.

"That's all I know," the server said, standing up. "I'm sorry."

"Wait," I said. "Downtown. You mean the police station?"

"Yes ma'am."

I stood up. "Can I walk there?"

The server shook his head. "I wouldn't recommend it. It's on the other side of town."

I pulled out my phone, opening my Uber app. I needed to get to the police station.

Although I had an Uber scheduled in the morning to

Denver, there was nothing available in Whiskey Springs tonight. Not one car.

I needed to get to the police station. I looked up to ask the server about other ways to get there, but he'd already left me, moved on to the next table.

I blew out a breath. I couldn't just sit back and let Wesley be arrested for protecting my honor. That was just wrong.

A customer walked through the door, letting in a blast of cold air. I couldn't go out dressed like this. Apparently it was a long walk and I would freeze without a coat.

I didn't have a really heavy coat with me, but I had one that would be better than the comparatively lightweight blazer I wore.

I dashed upstairs, grabbed my coat, and headed back down.

14

WESLEY

*T*wo hours later, the police gave me a ride back to the saloon in an unmarked car. I suppose I should have appreciated their consideration, but right now I wasn't feeling very appreciative of much of anything.

The car's headlights fought against the swirling mist that wasn't quite snow. Just a harbinger of bad weather to come.

It was a little late to get the bad weather I had wished so hard for. Now I didn't need it.

Isabella would have decided that I deserted her for reasons other than the truth. She would have no way to know what had happened to me.

Fortunately, they didn't want to put me in jail. Just questions. And a hefty fine.

I figured it would cost them more to keep me and they were all about collecting money, not spending it.

Still... I didn't trust them not to toss me in jail anyway. I had done the unthinkable.

So I had an order to return to court in two days. December 22. What kind of place held court two days before Christmas?

I tried to just pay it, but they weren't ready to let me off that easy. They wanted time to get the video footage from the saloon.

Seemed like a lot of trouble over a busted nose for a guy who deserved it. But when the guy with the busted nose was the police chief's son, well… all bets were off.

On top of everything else, I was going to have to call my parents and tell them I might not make it home for Christmas.

It didn't seem like a good idea to tell them why. I could tell them the flight was cancelled again. Things happened. I'd figure something out. Maybe the bad weather would hit Pittsburgh and I'd be off the hook.

The inside of the saloon looked significantly different than it had when I had been escorted out. The football game was over and the television was back to a normal volume level.

There were a couple of tables occupied by couples, deep in conversation with each other, ending the night the way I had hoped to end mine. With hope and maybe even promises.

But, of course, Isabella was no where to be seen.

She had no doubt left the saloon. Hell, I didn't even know if she was staying here. What were the odds of that? Too astronomical to compute.

I was halfway up the stairs when I saw her.

Isabella was sitting on the top step, a vantage point with a view of pretty much everything below, including the door.

I stopped right there on the stairs and just drank in the sight of her.

She was still wearing her pants suit and it was only then that I realized she was wearing black heeled pumps. The dark gray coat she wore was more suited to a southern climate than the mountain town of Whiskey Springs in December. She had no hat and no gloves. I don't know why that suddenly stood out to me, but it did.

"Hi," I said.

She stood up, took one step down. "I am so sorry," she said.

I shook my head. Did she know? How did she know?

"It's not your fault."

"I feel like it's my fault. I should have been the one to sock the jerk in the nose."

"Yeah," I said. "And then you would have been the one to be hauled downtown."

"Self-defense," she said with a little shrug.

I leaned against the railing. "Unfortunately, it's not that easy."

She lifted a delicate questioning brow.

"The jerk was the son of the Whiskey Springs police chief."

She slowly sat back down. Bit her lip. "I heard. You would think he would know better," she said.

"That's what I said." I walked up and sat down beside her.

She lowered her gaze and clasped her hands in her lap. "They told me not to go. To the police station." Then she looked up at me. "I wanted to."

I tucked a strand of hair behind her ear. "Oh. Love. They wouldn't have let you help me."

And I didn't want her down there anywhere near the police station. I didn't even like her being here in the saloon.

"So… they just let you go?"

"Not a chance. I have to go show up in court in two days."

"Here?" she asked.

"I have to cancel my flight out tomorrow." That part actually cheered me up a bit.

She was looking at me funny though. Like I had just said something in a foreign language.

"Are you staying here?" I asked.

She nodded.

"I need to get you to your room. It's getting a bit rowdy downstairs."

As much as I wanted to stay up all night talking to her, I was ready to call it a day and start over tomorrow.

15

ISABELLA

*W*esley was a perfect gentleman. He waited while I opened my door with the old-fashioned silver key.

"Goodnight," I said, over my shoulder as I stepped across the threshold.

"See you in the morning," he said.

I closed my door and leaned my cheek against the cool, smooth wood. It carried the scent of years. Hundreds of years of people coming and going.

I listened for his footsteps. For him to walk away. But I didn't hear them. I didn't hear him walk away.

Either he was still there or the old wooden door was uncommonly thick.

In the morning?

A simple phrase. Reassuring and optimistic.

He would be staying here for a court date in two days. But I had a flight scheduled out of here in the morning.

He'd said something that struck me as odd. He said he had to cancel his flight out of here in the morning.

There could be other flights, of course. There could be

another plane coming in for him. But there was the plane I had delivered today. And it was scheduled to go out in the morning. Was that the flight Wesley was supposed to be on? Was he a Skye Travels passenger?

There was always that possibility. But...out of all the people in Whiskey Springs, no matter how small a town it was...

I walked slowly to the armchair in front of the window and sat down.

Routinely checked to make sure my flight out of Denver was on time for tomorrow. Checked that my Uber was still confirmed to get me to the Denver Airport on time.

Everything was as it should be.

Except for me.

I wasn't as I should be.

First of all, Wesley had to stay here because of me. To show up in court. Because of me.

It wasn't like it was my fault, but it was still because of me.

He had come to my rescue.

I rubbed a hand over my arm where the jerk had grabbed me. It was already tender to the touch. I fully expected to have fingerprint bruises on my arm.

The jerk was the guy who should be punished. Not Wesley.

I straightened and embraced the indignation that swept over me.

Something needed to be done about this.

I couldn't just leave Wesley here to go to court on my behalf when he had hit the guy for my benefit. And I had only been a stranger to him at the time.

We still were technically strangers, but I felt a connection with Wesley.

I mentally went through my schedule for the next couple of days.

Tomorrow I had my trip on a commercial flight back to

Houston. So far, I didn't have any work flights scheduled until after Christmas.

Surely I was forgetting something. There was always a flight in there somewhere.

I opened my scheduling app and double-checked. I had remembered correctly. I had no flights scheduled until two days after Christmas.

It could always change, of course.

I rested my phone in my lap and looked outside at the full moon. A swirl of misty clouds drifted over it like a gossamer web.

The electric heat kicked on and I shivered.

I needed sleep.

I had a good reason for staying and supporting Wesley through this ordeal. I even had something of a moral obligation to stay here.

It was a good reason.

And second of all, he had called me *love*.

16

WESLEY

I slept about as well as I always did, which wasn't to say I slept very well at all.

I woke early, as usual. Had some coffee and toast sent up.

While I ate, I answered emails. Fielded problems.

Being the owner of a company meant I was ultimately responsible for all decisions. I had learned to delegate. Had gotten quite good at it, actually. But with the Christmas holidays, people were off. People were off, but the work continued. The owner of the company didn't get days off. Not really. I answered emails and questions no matter what time of the day or night as needed.

Most things could wait, but if there was an emergency, I was the one they called.

I didn't mind. Responsibility was part of being an entrepreneur. It was how I was able to live the lifestyle I lived. It was how I was able to charter a private jet anywhere I wanted to go around the country. And the reason I wasn't tied to a desk working for someone, living paycheck to paycheck.

Family was the only thing I hadn't been able to escape. It

was funny. I loved my family dearly. My parents. My two younger sisters.

But they didn't understand what I did. They lived a different lifestyle.

And somehow that made going home for Christmas a little more challenging each year.

It was no doubt me. My way of seeing the world.

I didn't see how they stayed there. Never venturing outside of their comfort zone.

My mother had been a school teacher in the same school, the same classroom, as a matter of fact, since before I was even born. One sister was following along in our mother's footsteps, just starting out teaching third grade. The other sister was still in school. About to graduate with a degree in finance. Would have been admirable except that she was planning to go to work at a local bank. Just like our father.

I was the only one in the family who had a compulsion to break the mold. It had been hard at first, but I had a tenaciousness that most people didn't.

I'd lost every friend I'd had from high school and even after that. Everyone seemed disappointed that I didn't just give up and take a "real" job.

Now I had employees. Now I was successful and I had freedom that none of those former friends had.

There was only one thing missing from my life. I didn't have a family of my own.

I was thirty-two years old and I was still single. I hadn't met that person I wanted to start a family with. To spend the rest of my life with. To grow old with.

I'd thought for a minute, maybe two, that Bailey was that someone for me. I'd even taken her home to meet my family.

And then it went south. Bailey and I didn't want the same things. And, of course, my family liked her, or at least liked the idea of her. So I had to deal with that when I got to Pittsburgh.

I sent a message to Skye Travels, explaining that something unforeseen had come up and I had to postpone my flight until possibly day after tomorrow. I would stay in touch. Let them know.

If I had left yesterday like I had planned, none of this would have happened. Right about now, I would be sitting in my parents' kitchen answering too many questions from my mother and sisters.

Powering off the computer, everything caught up for the moment, I checked the time.

It was time for me to shower and go downstairs to wait for Isabella. I knew which room she was in, but I wasn't going to knock on her door.

Still, I didn't want to risk missing her in case she happened to leave early.

Tomorrow I had to be present in court—for giving the police chief's son a bloody nose. In the light of day, I could think of so many better ways I could have handled the situation. More peaceful ways. More legal ways.

Something about that guy had brought out the worst in me. Or maybe it had something to do with Isabella.

When I saw her sitting there, something inside me had tripped. My heart rate had sped up. And I hadn't been able to take my eyes off her.

When I'd seen the jerk—his name was Calvin Wallace—put his hand on her arm and saw her alarmed expression, I'd felt a primal reaction. A reaction I couldn't remember having since I was a teenager.

It was unfortunate that my attraction to someone came along with the need to hit someone else.

But there was one thing I learned from this all this.

The old adage "be careful what you wish for" was still around for a reason.

I had wished for a reason to stay in Whiskey Springs.

And that was exactly what I had gotten.

Thirty minutes later, I found Isabella sitting at a table in the saloon. A red paper coffee cup on the table next to her, she sat with her hands clasped in her lap. A tote bag at her feet.

17

ISABELLA

I couldn't say that I knew what I was going to do. All I knew was that I felt compelled to get up earlier than planned to catch my flight.

My overnight bag held a pair of blue jeans, a t-shirt, and a sweatshirt. After getting dressed, I had braved an ice cold walk two doors down to a fancy coffee shop to buy myself a latte.

I didn't linger in the coffee shop though. I walked back out into the frigid cold and took my coffee back to the saloon, sat at one of the many empty tables.

The table I chose allowed me to see up the stairs, much as I had seen down the stairs last night from my perch on the top step.

The piano, thank goodness, sat quietly. No one pounding out Christmas songs. And the television was on the Denver news, the volume down low enough that it was merely background noise.

There were only a few people having breakfast at the tables. Breakfast, it seemed, was not nearly as popular a choice as dinner, at least not between six and seven a.m.

I sipped my coffee, but mostly I sat and waited.

My Uber was scheduled to pick me up outside the saloon at seven thirty. It was possible that Wesley would not come downstairs before then.

If he didn't, I would have to decide what I was going to do.

At six fifteen, I got a text from my brother. His scheduled passenger had delayed his flight until tentatively day after tomorrow. The Phenom was mine until then if I wanted it.

I blew out a breath and sat up straighter.

This changed things. I immediately texted back.

ME: *Thanks for the update. Canceling my commercial flight.*

I canceled my Uber first, then my flight. Flight was nonrefundable. I didn't care. I had options now.

I still didn't know what I was going to do, but at least now I didn't have to know. I had options.

When I caught sight of Wesley coming down the stairs, my breath hitched just a little.

I had thought about him all night. Couldn't stop. But seeing him again, this morning, I was surprised at how handsome he was. More handsome even than I remembered and I hadn't noticed the confidence he wore about him.

He reminded me of a pilot. Of the way he moved with the air of assurance. But he wasn't dressed like a pilot.

No, I decided, he wasn't a pilot, but was a man of success. Maybe even power.

I waited until he stopped in front of me.

"Good morning," he said with an amused little smile.

"Hi." I gestured for him to sit.

He pulled out a chair and sat down.

"Going somewhere?" he asked, nodding toward my tote bag, sitting next to my chair.

"Probably," I said. "I haven't decided yet."

"Sounds mysterious."

"A little, maybe." I shrugged and sat back, picked up my coffee cup.

0

KATHRYN KALEIGH

"Well," he said, sitting back. "I'm not going anywhere. At least not until day after tomorrow."

I cringed on the inside. "I know."

"And before you apologize, don't."

A server, a young lady I hadn't seen last night stopped at our table.

"Breakfast?" she asked.

He looked over at me questioningly.

"Wouldn't mind," I said.

"You, ah, have time?"

I nodded. "I can make time." I absolutely had time, but I decided that maybe I wouldn't tell him just yet.

From my first impression, Wesley was accustomed to getting what he wanted without much trouble.

It never hurt to be a bit of a challenge.

"Coffee," he said to the server. "Eggs, bacon, hashbrowns."

"I'll have the same," I said with a glance at the server. "But no coffee. Just water."

"At least we have breakfast," he said after the server left.

I hid a smile behind my coffee cup.

Yes. We had breakfast.

Then I definitely had to fly out of Whiskey Springs.

Away from this place that cast spells over my siblings, leading them to the marriage alter.

I was in no way looking for that for myself. Even if the man sitting across from me did have my heart racing a little too fast and even had me devising excuses to stay another night in Whiskey Springs.

18

WESLEY

I stood at the end of the mahogany bar and watched the conversation between Isabella and Stephen, the bartender/hotel clerk.

"You just checked out less than an hour ago," Stephen said.

"Then surely it's still available."

Stephen clicked computer keys. "I wish it was. Someone left early last night. But it's been reserved for three months. Coming in. Staying for a week."

She glanced at me. I just shrugged.

"What about another room?"

Stephen shook his head. "You got lucky last night. We stay booked up this time of year."

She nodded. "What about another hotel in town?"

Stephen just shook his head. "The whole town is booked up."

Isabella tapped her fingers on the bar. I could almost see her mind working. "A bed and breakfast?"

"Sorry."

"Okay," she said. "Thanks for your time."

Stephen looked at me and shrugged helplessly behind her back as she walked toward me.

I turned and we walked together back to our table.

"What now?" I asked.

"I don't know," she said with that thoughtful, contemplative expression.

"I guess you won't be staying in Whiskey Springs." I made the assumption that she had driven here and that's why she had the option of leaving or not.

She stared out the window as we sat in our chairs. "I can drive into Boulder. Spend the night." She looked back at me. "What time is court tomorrow?"

"Nine o'clock."

She cringed.

"There's no need for you to do that," I said. "They just want me to pay a hefty fine before I head out."

"Taking advantage of tourists," she said, her voice carrying a healthy dose of indignation.

"I guess so," I said. "I'm the one who hit him."

She smiled. "I still think he deserved it."

"He definitely deserved it."

"Being the police chief's son, especially."

"You would think," I said.

"So what are you going to do all day?"

"I don't really have anything planned," I said. "If it warms up, I might take a hike up to the falls."

"It's not going to warm up," she said, quickly, without any doubt.

"Well," I said. "I don't know what I'll do then."

She met my gaze. Looked at me with those sparkling deep green eyes. So deep and hinting of uncommon wisdom in a person so young.

"Do you want some company?" she asked. "Doing nothing."

I grinned. "Having company doing nothing is always nice."

She nodded and checked her phone.

"Are you sure you don't have anywhere to be?"

"I can always find somewhere to be," she said.

An odd statement, but she had me charmed.

"I guess here is just about as good a place to be as anywhere else."

"Kinda what I was thinking," she said. "Maybe I can distract you from being nervous about going to court."

"I'm not nervous," I said.

"You're a brave man," she said. "Small towns have their own way of doing things."

"I'm sure they do." Even despite my brave words, I felt a twinge of apprehension. She was right. Small town did have their own way of doing things.

I still didn't know what she was going to do about not having a place to stay.

I had some ideas, but she might not appreciate them.

Especially since they all involved kissing.

19

ISABELLA

*T*he sun cast a wash of gold through the clouds as it splashed over the tops of the snow-capped mountains. It tumbled over the mountains into the valley until it shone softly on Main Street. And with the soft glow of the just-risen sun, came a flurry of early-morning activity.

Mostly people heading into the coffee shop. Some stopping by the saloon for a hearty breakfast.

Wesley and I had moved over to sit on a bench in front of the fireplace. The roaring fire crackled behind us, warming our backs.

I faced a quandary.

I now had options. Almost more options than I knew what to do with.

I'd planned on catching a flight—a commercial flight—back to Houston today. That had been my original plan.

I had not planned on meeting Wesley. I certainly had not been planning on Wesley having to go to court for defending me.

The logical answer was for me to catch a ride to the Whiskey Springs airport and fly the Phenom back to Houston.

The downside to that was either I or someone else would still have to return it.

The thought of coming back was compelling. Especially if my hunch was right and Wesley was the passenger my brother was supposed to have been flying out today. Otherwise it was all one big coincidence and I wasn't inclined to believe that. If I believed that, it was just a slippery slope to believing in that magic of Whiskey Springs that my siblings all claimed.

I could just ask him if he was a Skye Travels client, but I didn't feel like I knew him quite well enough. People who flew by private jet were a different type of people. And if I was wrong, well… I didn't want to make things awkward.

And besides that, I wasn't ready to tell him I was a pilot.

My illogical—gut—answer was to stay here and go to court with him.

Then again, I could fly to Houston, pick up some clothes—

My phone chimed, interrupting the tangle of thoughts that swirled unproductively in my head.

Momma: *Good morning. Are you on your way home yet?*

Momma always started her text conversations with a greeting. She'd learned that from her mother. Neither one of them realized that text messages were like ongoing conversations that didn't really start or end.

"It's my mother," I said, meeting Wesley's sparkling blue eyes. He always seemed to be looking at me when I looked at him. And it didn't seem to bother him that I caught him looking at me.

"Uh oh. I'm always in trouble when my mother messages me."

I laughed. "It's because you're a boy," I said. "And boys always are in trouble."

He just lifted an eyebrow. "Can't say you're wrong on that one."

ME: *Not yet. Trying to decide if I want to stay here a couple of days.*

MOMMA: *I thought you were afraid to go near Whiskey Springs.*

Sometimes I talked too much.

ME: *Not afraid. Just wary.*

MOMMA: *Daniel and Jenna need to fly to Denver to pick up some decorations for tonight's Christmas decorating thing.*

My family used airplanes like most people used cars. While most people would jump in the car to drive the couple of hours into Denver, my family jumped in a plane.

"Everything okay?" Wesley asked.

Thought bubbles.

"I think so. Tonight there's a Christmas tree decorating thing?"

Wesley shrugged. "I don't know. Maybe."

MOMMA: *Would you drop them off on your way out?*

Maybe. If I was sure I was going that way.

ME: *How will they get home?*

MOMMA: *IDK*

I rolled my eyes. Momma rarely worried about anything.

ME: *I'll take them. But he could have asked me himself.*

MOMMA: *I'm sure he would have. But since it was my idea...*

I looked over at Wesley. He smiled.

I liked his smile. And his eyes. I really had nothing to lose. And this way I had every excuse to stay over and go to court with Wesley.

It was almost like my decision had been made for me.

"I have to run an errand." I told him. "Do you want to come with me?"

"Okay. Where are we going?"

"Denver."

20

WESLEY

*I*sabella's trip to Denver was not what I expected.

The Uber driver dropped us at the Whiskey Springs airport and drove off, leaving us standing in what was basically the middle of nowhere.

The terminal was locked up, apparently not completely staffed yet. It was my understanding that it was a new airport.

The terminal building itself, resembling a big log cabin, blended in well with the surrounding forest.

When she'd said she had to run an errand, to Denver, I had expected us to be taking a road trip. I had been surprised when we had gone to the airport instead.

I had been even more surprised when the airplane sitting on the tarmac was a Skye Travels airplane. I knew from the red Skye Travels logo splashed across the plane.

"Are we early?" I asked. Two chipmunks skittered across the parking lot and a couple of blackbirds landed right in front of us, begging for food.

It was a beautiful day. Perfect for flying. The swirling mist from the morning had burned off in the sunlight, leaving just wispy white clouds high in the sky.

"Not really," she said, walking straight over to the airplane.

I stood watching another car coming toward us when I heard the door to the airplane open.

By the time I looked back, Isabella had the steps down and was inside the plane.

I hurried to catch up.

"Are you a stewardess?" I asked.

She gave me a look. "They're called flight attendants now," she said. "And no."

I followed her to the cockpit, wondering if we were doing something illegal. I already had one court appointment. Didn't need two.

"You can sit next to me," she said as she plopped down into the pilot's seat.

As I stood watching her, I heard two car doors open outside.

Holding a headset in one hand, she looked over at me with a warning glance. "If you don't sit here, my brother will and you'll miss out."

Not wanting to miss out on anything, I sat in the copilot's chair.

I'd flown in cockpits before, but never in a Phenom. Most just smaller jets. This airplane was impressive. Three computer screens across the front and more buttons and knobs than I could count.

She held up a second headset for me to put on. "Do you know how to buckle up?" she asked.

"I think I can manage."

She made quick introductions when the two passengers came aboard.

"Hello Daniel. Hi Jenna. This is Wesley. He's going to be flying with us today."

"We've met," Daniel said.

"He was my pilot coming in," Wesley said as he secured his four-point harness.

"Do you mind closing the door?" Isabella asked.

"Guess not," Daniel said, then turned to his wife. "Looks like we're passengers today."

"I don't mind," Jenna said. "We can make out while your sister does the driving."

"Have I ever told you how lucky I am to have found you?" Daniel asked as the door slid into place and locked.

"Just ignore them," Isabella said. "They're newlyweds."

"A little hard to ignore," I said, but she was right. This was going to be interesting.

And ten minutes later, we were in the air.

There was something most decidedly sexy about a female pilot.

And to think that I had not known that particular piece of trivia until now.

21

ISABELLA

*T*his day was turning out far better than I had expected when I had gotten up this morning.

Not only was I getting to fly, but I was sitting next to Wesley.

At the moment, at least, having Wesley sitting next to me trumped my trepidation about being anywhere near the magic spell of Whiskey Springs.

After navigating the mountains, I leveled off at five thousand feet. Denver was too close to take the plane much higher.

"You were supposed to be on this flight," I said. It was a statement. Not a question. I saw his name on the log. My hunch had been right.

"If not for Calvin Wallace," I said.

"Also known as the jerk," she said.

"I think they made a movie about him, didn't they?"

"I think you're right," I said with a little chuckle.

I checked gauges and scowled when I spotted the potential for turbulence ahead.

"Turbulence ahead," I said into the microphone, knowing my brother didn't need an explanation.

"How do you know?" Wesley asked.

"See that little pocket," I pointed to a spot on the radar.

"Not really." He leaned forward, trying to see what I saw.

"Hold on," I said just as the plane dropped.

I gritted my teeth. The one thing I did not like about the mountains. Turbulence. The Phenom could handle it. I had no doubt. Didn't take away the shock of dropping several feet in the air.

"You okay?" I asked, glancing over at Wesley.

"Couldn't be better," he said, but he wasn't looking at me now. He was looking straight ahead and his knuckles clenched the arms of the chairs were white.

"Don't worry," I said. "It's perfectly normal and safe."

"I know," he said. "Doesn't take away the shock value."

I was beginning to think that Wesley and I were kindred spirits.

"Do you fly?" I asked. "I mean, are you a pilot?"

"Never had the time or the inclination. I typically use flying time to get some work done."

I nodded. "Most people do."

It was time to begin our descent into Denver. I needed all my attention focused on the flight.

After getting permission from the control tower to go in for a landing, I spotted the runway up ahead.

"Prepare to land," I said in the microphone, then to Wesley. "Almost there."

"Quick flight."

"A lot faster than driving."

I focused on the landing. I could land a plane in my sleep— and often did go through the motions in my dreams, but one misstep could lead to disaster, so I put all my attention on the airplane and runway. Every flight... every landing... was different.

As the wheels touched the runway, I let out a little sigh of relief.

"Nice landing," Wesley said.

"Thanks."

"You're good."

"You sound surprised."

"I'm still getting used to the idea of you being a pilot."

I grinned.

People rarely noticed the landing or the flight at all for that matter as long as everything went smoothly. It was when things went wrong that people noticed.

It was nice to have someone appreciate a smooth landing.

I could get used to having Wesley along.

And now that we weren't in Whiskey Springs at the moment, I didn't have to worry about the little town's propensity to cast a spell on people that led them to get married.

After unharnessing and going to open the door, I noticed that my sister-in-law's hair was a bit mussed.

I glanced over at Wesley and rolled my eyes.

He just grinned.

Boys.

22

WESLEY

I was a bit jealous of Isabella's brother. I'd enjoyed sitting next to her in the cockpit during the flight, but Daniel and Jenna had obviously had a more intimate kind of enjoyment.

Must be nice to have pilots in the family.

I had flown with Daniel Fleming before. He was a good pilot.

It was interesting that Skye Travels would hire siblings like this. In the corporate world, it was frowned upon. And I would bet money that having two siblings on the same flight would have been against the rules most places.

But then from what I knew about Noah Worthington, he did whatever he wanted to do. And did it with boldness and success.

He had actually been one of my role models when I had been starting out with my own company.

It was interesting how things came around. He'd been my role model and now I was using his services.

Daniel sat in the front seat of the taxi, while Isabella

climbed in the back and sat in the middle. Jenna sat next to her on one side. So I slid into place on her right.

Daniel chatted with the taxi driver, but the three of us sat quietly in the back. The taxi was a bit older. A bit ragged. But it had a safe, familiar feel to it.

As we turned a corner, Isabella slid next to me and I reflexively put an arm over the seat behind her.

Even though her head only bumped my shoulder for a couple of seconds, I realized she was more petite than I'd noticed.

She smelled like a swirl of wildflowers and vanilla mixed with an undertone of jet fuel. It was funny, really. I had never, ever imagined myself being attracted to a woman who smelled anything like jet fuel.

I'd grown up in an upper middle-class household. A family of bankers and school teachers. I had dated the prom queen in high school. She had been the feminine of feminine girls and had set the tone for girls I was attracted to over the years after that.

Bailey, my last girlfriend, had specialized in fashion. She could spot a designer handbag from across the room. Spent hours in the salon, to achieve the perfect blend of blonde highlights. Her idea of an ideal date was flowers, wine, and a walk through a museum or sitting in a symphony. I could never see her in a cockpit flying an airplane.

The idea of it was so out of character, it almost made me laugh out loud.

And yet Isabella—if I was any judge at all—had natural uncolored brunette hair and her smile was more beautiful than Bailey's. Isabella's smile was a genuine smile with her eyes.

Not to compare, but the contrast in their interests was so remarkably different I had a little trouble wrapping my head around it.

The driver navigated onto the freeway. Denver traffic was,

as always, hopelessly congested. We headed northeast into the fray of it.

"We should get lunch first," Jenna suggested.

Daniel and Isabella proceeded to have a conversation about where we should eat lunch.

When Isabella smiled up at me, my heart went into a tailspin.

I'd already been attracted to her, but there was something about the way she looked at me. Almost in a way that suggested that she and I shared some kind of secret.

And I found that irresistible. I knew in that moment that I had fallen off the cliff. Head over heels in love with Isabella Fleming.

And the thing about it was, I didn't mind it not even just one bit.

23

ISABELLA

While my brother and his wife walked around the huge craft store filling a cart with everything Christmas, Wesley and I were left to entertain ourselves.

"What do you think their theme is?" he asked, watching them examine decorations and tossing them in the cart.

I scrunched my nose. "You think they have one?"

He laughed. "Yes. I do. I think it's Christmas."

"Interesting theme." I nodded, keeping a straight face.

We turned and walked in the opposite direction, but there was no escaping the brightly colored, festive Christmas decorations.

"What were Christmases like when you were growing up?" I asked.

As we walked in front of a row of a display of full-length decorative mirrors for sale, I glimpsed our reflection.

Wesley and I made a nice looking couple. He was about a head taller than me and we just looked like we fit together.

But it wasn't just our physical appearance. We got along. Being with Wesley was... easy. In a good way.

"Typical, I guess," he said. "Small family. With two younger sisters, I was always recruited to help build things."

"What kinds of things did you build?" I picked up a stuffed cat wearing a Santa outfit. Set it back down.

"You know. Dollhouses. The usual girl stuff."

I didn't know. Our dollhouses always came already built.

"I'm the youngest of five," I said. "So I guess I was on the other end of all that."

Wesley stopped in the middle of the aisle and looked at me. "Five? There are five of you?"

"Yeah. I come from a rather large family." That was probably an understatement and I knew it. Now that my cousins were getting married and having children, it was getting rather hard to keep up.

"What was that like?" he asked, walking in step with me again.

"Not so different, probably," I said, picking up a glittery star tree topper and holding it up to the light. "Except for Christmas Eve. On Christmas Eve the whole extended family gets together at my grandparents' house. It seems like there are more people every year."

"How many of your brothers and sisters are married?"

I looked across the store at my brother and Jenna. They were laughing at something and already they had started on filling the second cart.

"All of them," I said, looking away.

"You have a lot of in-laws."

I laughed. "You're not kidding. But you know… I like all of them."

"I hope I'm as fortunate when my sisters get married," he said. He too, was watching my brother, and there was a wistfulness in his tone that touched me. I didn't ask, but I wondered where that was coming from.

"Me too," I said, putting the glittery star down. I had no

need for any Christmas decorations. I liked Christmas as well as anyone else, but I didn't decorate my apartment. I was rarely home, so I had no need to.

My grandparents and my parents decorated enough for everyone. And I always spent the night at either my parents' house or my grandparents' house on Christmas.

I looked back at my brother and I wondered. I just wondered.

What would it be like to have a family of my own to spend Christmas with?

Even more, I wondered, shifted my gaze to Wesley, what would it be like to spend Christmas with him?

I shook my head. He wasn't a puppy. I couldn't just keep him.

Besides… just because we weren't in Whiskey Springs right now, didn't mean I didn't have to be careful.

There was definitely something about the air in that little town that I needed to be wary of.

I might be getting a little too attached to him. Especially since after tomorrow, I had to let him go.

24

WESLEY

J'd heard the expression *buying out the store*, but I'd never seen anyone actually do it until I saw the taxi's trunk crammed full of bags of decorations.

Daniel and Jenna had bought more decorations than they could possibly need.

Isabella stood, her hands on her hips, watching Daniel and me unload the airplane, moving everything to the rental car. They were standing close enough that I caught most of their conversation.

"How many trees do you have to decorate?" she asked.

"Just one," Jenna said. She stood sipping a milk shake.

Isabella turned to her sister-in-law. "So what are you going to do with the rest of all this?"

Jenna shrugged. "We'll just donate it."

"I see," Isabella said, noncommittally.

"Are you flying back to Houston tonight?" Jenna asked.

"I don't know yet," Isabella said. "I don't think there are any rooms in Whiskey Springs."

"You could stay with us," Jenna said, "but we're in my parents' house right now."

"I know," I said. "I'll figure something out."

"You can always crash on the couch."

"Thanks," Isabella said. "But I think I'll just fly back to Denver and get a room."

It was almost four o'clock.

The Fleming family had an odd sense of time. Jenna and Daniel had about one hour to get to the town's high school gym and get a tree decorated.

Isabella was talking about flying to Denver to spend the night because there weren't any rooms in Whiskey Springs. I suppose that meant she would get up in the morning and fly *back* to Whiskey Springs. To me, that sounded not only exorbitant, but also like a huge waste of time.

I'd already decided that she could take my room. I just wasn't going to offer it in front of her brother. It seemed disrespectful.

I hoped she would take it. The problem was then I would have no place to sleep. It was easier for me, though. I could sleep downstairs in the saloon. On the floor, if need be.

By the time we got back to the high school gym and carted everything inside, the place was crawling with people of all ages. Children racing around, squealing with delight when they caught sight of Santa walking around, trailed by a following of elves handing out little gift bags. Older couples, wandering about admiring the different Christmas trees—twelve of them scattered around the gym.

Walking through the gym was like walking through a sparkly, twinkling Christmas forest.

I wondered how much work must have gone into all this.

Whiskey Springs truly was synonymous with Christmas. I'd heard people say that, but now that I was seeing all this, I actually believed it.

Most everyone else seemed to already have their trees decorated or else they were finishing up. It was going to be interesting to see Jenna and Daniel decorate a tree in less than one hour.

"Come with me?" Isabella said. "Let's get some hot chocolate."

"Of course."

We made our way across the floor to an old-fashioned cart with an old-fashioned sign identifying it as Smedley's Ice Cream Shop. There was only one girl behind the counter and she was slammed.

"They're supposed to have hot chocolate floats," Isabella said as we got into line. There were about six people in front of us.

I looked at her sideways. "Hot chocolate ice cream? That's not a thing."

She smiled and lifted an eyebrow. "It's a thing in Whiskey Springs."

"Is that so?"

She took a deep breath, glanced around, then her gaze landed on mine and held.

"There are lots of things in Whiskey Springs."

"Like what?"

She shrugged. "I've heard people say that it has magic, especially this time of year."

"Do you believe that?" I asked.

"I don't not believe it," she said, still looking up at me.

I nodded.

With twinkling Christmas lights all around us mixed with soft music behind the happy tenor of conversations, I realized that I believed in the magic of Whiskey Springs.

And the funny thing was about all of this was that I had ended up here by chance. I wasn't supposed to be in Whiskey Springs at all.

25

ISABELLA

*N*ot surprisingly, Daniel and Jenna hadn't won the Christmas decorating contest. Not even an honorable mention. Apparently, eclectic wasn't a popular theme this year.

But they did win the appreciation of the townspeople when they spread dozens of random Christmas decorations on a table and gave them to anyone who wanted them.

I would have saved them for next year, or maybe even returned them, but I had to admit it was nice seeing how happy people seemed to be about getting a little unexpected gift.

Wesley and I sat on one of the benches, staying out of the way, but watching the festivities.

"You can have my room tonight," he said, out of the blue.

"What do you mean?"

"You can stay in my room and I'll sleep somewhere else."

"There isn't anywhere else," I said. "unless you know something I don't."

"I can sleep on the floor in the saloon."

"You can't do that." I said, looking at him sideways. "I'll sleep on Jenna's parents' couch." I didn't want to be an imposition, but since I'd already flown to Denver and back today, it didn't make sense to do it again.

"Okay," he said. "but I really think you should take my room."

"Why is that?" I asked, looking at him.

"So I can feel chivalrous," he said.

I laughed. "You've already rescued me once. We saw how that turned out. Besides. I think you've done more than your share."

"A man can never be overly chivalrous."

Someone turned off the music, signaling that it was time for everyone to start making their way out of the gym. We didn't move.

"Who told you that?"

"I don't know. I think I read it someplace."

"I think you made it up." I twisted the cap off my bottle of water and finished it off.

"Maybe."

"You think they want us to leave?" I asked, leaning back and crossing my ankles.

"I've never shut down a high school gym before."

"Sounds like a new experience for both of us." I glanced at my phone. "I'll text Jenna. Let her know I'm coming by." Wesley was staring straight ahead. His brow furrowed.

"But I left my overnight bag at the saloon."

"Want to have a drink while we're there?" he asked, looking back at me. He still looked at little troubled, but his eyes were smiling.

I calculated my next flight. Since I was going to court with him in the morning, the earliest I would be flying would be tomorrow afternoon.

That would be more than twelve hours bottle to throttle.

"Okay," I said, tucking a strand of hair behind my ear and looking up at him with a little smile.

He smiled back, then stood up and held out a hand.

"Shall we make these people happy then and get out of here?"

"Sure," I said, putting my hand in his.

As I stood and walked toward the door, still hand in hand with Wesley, I had the oddest sensation wash over me.

The sensation slid through me, lodging in my stomach, letting loose a kaleidoscope of butterflies.

And I knew right then that it didn't matter where we were or what we did as long as I was with Wesley.

It was such an overwhelming feeling that I nearly lost my balance.

And I knew I was in trouble.

I kept walking, my hand still in his, but my mind was stunned.

I had to do something.

I had fallen under the magical spell of Whiskey Springs.

26

WESLEY

I knew the moment something changed with Isabella. But for the life of me, I didn't know why.

We were one of the last ones to leave the gym/Christmas tree forest. It was different without the Christmas music—just echoed like any other high school gym.

When we stepped out into the cold, I unwrapped the scarf around my neck and placed it around hers.

"Thank you," she said, but her smile was different. I blamed it on the shards of cold wind slamming into our faces as we turned right to make the walk down Main Street to the saloon.

Main Street was still alive with people and music streaming from the speakers, blending with the different songs spilling out of the stores.

It was such a surprisingly happy, idyllic scene. One that stabbed a man right in the heart. There was nothing like this in Pittsburgh or any of the other many places I had visited.

Isabella had her hands stuffed in her coat pockets. I almost slipped my hand in the crook of her arm, but something in her expression stopped me.

She stared straight ahead, an expression of consternation on her face.

"Everything okay?" I asked.

"Yes," she said, with a small glance and a tight smile in my direction. Then she adjusted my scarf around her chin and seemed to huddle deeper inside her coat if that was possible.

I chose to believe that it was the cold. We had been getting along so well all day. Last night, too. I couldn't imagine that anything had changed.

Nothing had changed.

She hadn't gotten any text messages...

But she had sent Jenna a text. Maybe while she had her phone open she had seen another message from someone else.

It was possible.

I opened the door to the saloon and we stepped inside into the welcome warmth. By tacit agreement, we walked straight over to the bench in front of the fireplace. The best seat in the house.

She held her hands out to the flames, warming them. At least I knew why she didn't have a proper coat or gloves or a scarf. She hadn't been planning on doing anything more than just dropping off the plane and flying out the next morning.

"Are you sure you're okay?" I asked, reaching over to sweep a strand of hair aside so I could see her face.

She looked up at me and our eyes held. Her deep green eyes locked onto mine and seemed to see into my very soul.

"Isabella," I said softly.

Her lips parted and for just a split second, I could lean forward just a little and kiss her.

But an instant before I could—between the split second I realized the possibility and could have carried it out, she turned away, staring straight into the flames.

She sat for a moment, fidgeting, her legs bouncing up and down.

I ran a hand over my chin and struggled to figure out what had happened.

I replayed our recent conversations.

And came up empty-handed.

I couldn't think of anything that would have caused this quick change. She would hardly look at me.

"I have to go," she said, standing up suddenly.

"Why? Where?"

Not looking at me, she just shook her head. After a quick stop by the bar to grab her overnight bag, she practically ran to the door.

I watched as she turned right. I didn't know if I should follow her or just let her go.

I couldn't make sense of it. I was at a complete loss.

Sitting here, alone, in front of the fire, I realized I didn't even have her phone number.

27

ISABELLA

*A*s I looked into Wesley's sparkling blue eyes, I felt off balance and couldn't focus my thoughts.

With the warm flames of the crackling fire in front of us, reflecting in his eyes, he almost kissed me. Almost.

Half a second more and he would have done just that.

And I would have let him.

Then I'd heard the bartender clinking glasses against each other and somehow it had jarred a memory from the back of my mind.

Daniel. Makenna. Jack. Greyson.

All four of my older siblings had traveled here to Whiskey Springs for one reason or another and every one of them had married someone they met here. Someone who had a tie to here.

Daniel and Jenna were building a house here.

Makenna and Charlie lived in Houston.

Jack (Dr. Fleming) and Bella lived here.

Greyson and Noelle, newlyweds, hadn't figured out what they were going to do yet. Noelle was genuinely a princess, giving them more options than they knew what to do with.

So the five of us siblings had talked. Actually they had talked. I had listened. And they had all decided that Whiskey Springs held some kind of magic that brought soul mates together.

Their conversation was quite frankly terrifying. To think that just coming here to this quaint little town in the mountains would somehow unite me with my soulmate struck fear in my heart.

It wasn't that didn't want to meet my soulmate and get married. I did.

I just somehow thought that I would meet him by accident. And sparks would fly.

Thinking that I would meet him here in Whiskey Springs seemed predestined and that was scary. I felt like it took away my choices.

And I liked to make my own decisions.

And I wanted to stay in Houston. I was debating between buying a condo in our family high rise or buying a two-story condo on the ground.

I could admit I was stalling about that. And maybe I was waiting until I found someone I could make those decisions with.

It was something of a contradiction to being independent, but some things were just more fun to do with someone else. For instance, that someone who would be sharing the condo with me.

And, damn it, I kept thinking about Wesley being that someone sharing a home… a life… with me.

We had had such a good day together today. Just an easy day. He was easy to be around. Comfortable. And at the same time… when I looked into his eyes, my thoughts scattered and drunken butterflies erupted in my stomach.

My hands shook, even now as I headed toward Jenna's

parents' house. I didn't look over my shoulder. If Wesley followed me, I didn't want to know it.

I didn't want to be tempted to stop and turn around.

If he wasn't following me, I didn't want to know that either. I didn't want to know that he would just let me walk away without a fight.

Reaching Jenna's door, I barely knocked before Daniel opened it.

Stepping inside, I didn't even ask where Jenna was. My eyes stung. From the cold. It was definitely from the cold. Definitely not from my utter confusion over Wesley.

"Where's Wesley?" he asked.

"He has a room at the saloon," I said, moving to take off my scarf.

But it wasn't my scarf. It was Wesley's scarf.

And it smelled like him. It smelled masculine. Leather and deeply earthly.

With a sigh, I stopped, my hands still on the scarf, and looked at my brother.

"I hate Whiskey Springs," I said.

When Daniel laughed, I scowled at him.

He thought I was kidding.

I wasn't even supposed to be in Whiskey Springs, much less fall in love.

28

WESLEY

*T*he saloon was crowded, much as it had been last night. But tonight, I wasn't interested in people watching. No interest whatsoever. I didn't even want to know if there was a damsel in distress. If there was, she would not be my damsel. Not this time.

Piano music blended with the weather channel on the television. No football game tonight. Just weather. Everyone was watching to see if there was even the slightest chance of a white Christmas.

I had what I considered the best seat in the house—right in front of the fireplace. But now that Isabella had left, she had taken the warmth and light with her, leaving my world a dull gray.

It didn't take much effort to figure out where Isabella was going. I knew she was going to Jenna's parents' house to stay with her brother and sister-in-law.

And since he was my pilot, I had Daniel's phone number.

ME: *I think Isabella is on her way there.*

DANIEL: *You're welcome to come, too.*

ME: *I know.*

Thought bubbles.

DANIEL: *Something happened?*

I knew what he was asking. Isabella and I had been inseparable all day. It didn't make sense that she would suddenly take off by herself.

ME: *Not sure. Just make sure she gets there.*

DANIEL: *Walking up the sidewalk now.*

ME: *Thanks.*

I dropped my phone in my lap. Even Daniel found it odd that Isabella would go off without me.

I didn't know what she and I had, but we had something.

Even if I couldn't figure it out, I would have to figure out what to do about it.

But for now, I needed to focus on getting ready for my defense tomorrow.

So I did what I usually did when I traveled. I ordered a glass of wine and took it with me to my room. I settled into the bed, turned on the television, and picked up the novel I was reading.

At least I knew how to get in touch with Isabella's brother. It was a relief knowing that I could at least find her.

The only problem was she didn't appear to want to see me.

And, for the life of me, I couldn't figure out why.

I set the novel aside. I wasn't reading a single word anyway.

She had first started acting different in the gym. When we were talking about closing it down before we decided to leave.

It seemed innocuous enough. Playful even.

Then I'd taken her hand and we had walked across the gym toward the door, hand in hand. It had just felt natural. And, maybe subconsciously it had been my way of claiming her as mine. She'd had one run in with a fellow from here. Was that just last night? And I didn't care to have anyone else think they could be laying a claim to her.

It was very Neanderthal.

And very unlike me.

I was just a regular guy who happened to be very persistent, which allowed me to be successful in my business.

Maybe I needed to apply some of that persistence to my personal life. To Isabella.

I just had to come up with a logical and purposeful strategy.

Maybe I didn't need to know what had led to her sudden change in demeanor.

Maybe I just needed to know how to fix it.

29

ISABELLA

*a*t six o'clock the next morning, I stood in front of Jenna's open closet. Clothes neatly organized and sorted.

"You can borrow whatever you like," she said. "My business clothes are on the right. I hardly ever wear anything but the shirts on days I have to record an online lecture."

Jenna was a former college professor turned online professor. I didn't want to tell her, but what she considered business clothes were actually rather casual in my world.

It was okay. It was just court in Whiskey Springs. I could even wear my blue jeans and sweatshirt and no one would think anything about it. I just happened to have a personal thing about not wearing clothes more than one day without laundering them.

Fortunately Jenna and I happened to be close enough to the same size that I could wear her clothes.

"What do you suggest wearing to a court hearing?" I asked, one hand on my hip while I tried not to think about the real reason I wanted to look nice. That I would be seeing Wesley.

"I think you wear whatever you want to wear," Jenna said.

Something in her voice caught my attention.

"Are you okay?" I asked. Her eyes were closed and she looked a little green around the gills.

She held up a hand. "I'll be right back," she said.

Turning around swiftly, she left her room and dashed down the hall.

I slid hangers along the bar, looking for something black. Finding a plain black sheath dress with long sleeves, I pulled it out and held it up against me. The length wasn't bad. Just above my knees.

Moving to her shirts and blazers, I found a short red blazer that suited me. Since it was Christmas, I decided, it was perfect.

Jenna came back.

"Are you okay?"

"Yeah," she said. "I think I just ate something that didn't agree with me."

"Oh." I laid the clothes on the bed and studied Jenna. She was from a small family. I, on the other hand, had more cousins than I could count. And those cousins were getting married and having babies.

"Jenna?" I wasn't sure it was my place to point out the obvious.

She was studying the clothes I had laid on the bed. "This should look good on you."

When her gaze darted back to mine, I put a hand on her elbow.

"Do you think you might be pregnant?" I asked.

Jenna's eyes widened and a flurry of emotions washed over her face.

"Maybe," she said, on a whisper.

I nodded matter-of-factly. "I'll grab a pregnancy test at the drug store on the way back."

Jenna nodded too, her eyes moist with unshed tears.

I was happy for her. And my brother. She made him happy.

This would be my first niece or nephew. I drew her into a hug. "This is wonderful news."

"We need the test," Jenna said, inhaling sharply.

She was such a scientist.

"We'll have it soon. And then you can go see Jack. He can make it official." My brother, Dr. Jack Fleming, had an office just off of Main Street a few blocks away. He was currently in Houston, but I didn't see the need to point out that particular detail.

"Right," she said, taking a ragged breath. "Our house isn't ready yet." Obviously overwhelmed, Jenna sat down on the armchair and looked at me. "We're not ready."

"It's okay," I said. "Trust me. Everything will come together. No one is ever ready when it happens, but life shifts and accommodates. You'll see."

"Thank you," Jenna said. "You're the best sister-in-law."

I grinned. "I'm going to get dressed. See how this looks on me."

Leaving her alone for a few minutes would give her time to absorb this life changing news. She looked a little stunned. Stunned but happy.

And I was going to be an aunt.

What they called a maiden aunt. Well, I decided, as I pulled on the skirt and zipped it in the back, I would be the best maiden aunt possible. Gifts. Trips. They would love me.

Even if I never married, my siblings could name children after me.

I pulled on my blazer and looked at myself in the mirror. The dress fit perfectly and molded just right to my figure.

Was that how I really wanted to live my life? Did I want to be a genealogical orphan?

Of course not. No one wanted that. Just because I didn't want to get married *right now*, didn't mean I never wanted to get married.

And once again, Wesley's face flashed through my mind.

Whiskey Springs.

There was something going on with this place.

Something that let butterflies loose in my stomach and distorted my normal way of thinking.

30

WESLEY

*M*y court appointment was a bit anticlimactic. The courtroom, about the size of any typical waiting room, with six rows of plastic chairs, was scattered with people waiting to pay their fines.

I had no reason to think it was anything more. Everything else was just for show. Like me having to show up here today. I should have been allowed to just pay the fine and go about my way. I couldn't be upset about it though. If not for this court date, I would have flown out yesterday and missed my time with Isabella.

When it was my turn to approach the bench, I was asked a few questions which I contritely answered. I'd been wrong to hit him and I knew it.

The judge was a middle-aged woman with flat affect, but she worked with efficiency. She assigned my fine and advised me to keep my hands to myself in the future.

I took my paperwork and turned to leave.

The judge, unceremoniously moved on to the next person.

At first I thought I must be imagining things. But when

Isabella didn't vanish after I blinked rapidly, I knew she was really here.

She looked serene. Her lightweight wool coat folded neatly in her lap. She was wearing a skirt and a candy apple red jacket. Her hair was pulled back, leaving a few strands framing her face.

My heart skipped a beat.

I grinned and she smiled back.

Taking my paperwork with me, I walked over and sat next to her. I still had to stop by the front desk and hand over my credit card, but seeing Isabella washed this whole experience away like a breath of fresh wind coming in from the mountains.

"You're here," I said.

"I told you I would be here," she said.

"There was nothing you could have done," I said. "It was just like I thought. Show up. Pay a fine."

"I know. But it's good to have a friend here anyway."

I placed a hand over hers and smiled to myself. She thought of herself as my friend. It wasn't exactly what I was aiming for, but it was in the right direction.

"I need to go pay this, then do you want to get some lunch?"

"It's a little early for lunch," she said.

I glanced at my watch. "A little." I shrugged. "We can take our time getting there. Check out some of the shops."

"Okay. I need to pick something up anyway," she said.

"Alright then." I stood up. Glanced over my shoulder at the officials sitting behind the bench. "It's time to get out of here."

She stood up and followed me out the door. The guard standing at the door nodded as we passed through.

"How did you get past the guard?" I asked, remembering how I'd had to show my identification and be screened with a metal detecting wand. And that was after showing my court order.

She lifted a brow. "I have skills."

"I'm sure you do," I said as she stood to the side while I went up to the checkout desk to pay my fine. I had a feeling they did this every day all day long. I was just one of many.

A few minutes later, as we stepped outside, I saw that Isabella was wearing my scarf beneath her coat.

I took that as a good sign that whatever had been bothering her yesterday had resolved itself.

We reached Main Street and blended in with the tourists walking up and down the street. I'm not sure why, but I didn't think of us as tourists. It was an odd phenomenon.

"Do you know any good places to eat besides the saloon?" I asked.

"Yes. Jenna suggested a restaurant called the Hungry Biscuit."

"Alright then." I assumed we'd come across it. But in the meantime, it was a nice walk along the street, the Christmas music streaming from the speakers.

There was an excited kind of energy in the air that came with the season.

"I need to stop in here for a minute," Isabella said as we passed by what looked like a drug store, but the sign over the door identified it as the *General Store*.

We stepped inside the store that had everything. Regular drug store items. Also souvenirs including t-shirts and mugs. A *Soda Fountain*.

When I stopped to study the soda fountain, Isabella dashed off in another direction. "I'll be right back," she said.

"Do you want me to—"

"Give me just a minute," she said over her shoulder.

I shrugged and admired the vintage soda fountain. It had red bar stools and the young man behind the counter wore a white cap that reminded me of old movies.

"Can I get you anything?" the lad asked.

"No. I'm just…" I caught sight of Isabella standing in line at the pharmacy check out. "Thank you though." I took off to catch up with her.

She had her back to me as she stepped up to the counter.

Something made me stop. Maybe it wasn't my business.

But then her cell phone rang. She held up a finger to the checker. "I'm sorry. I need to grab this. Can you just—?"

"Take your time," the young lady, probably a college student said.

Holding the phone to her ear, Isabella turned away.

I didn't mean to hear her conversation. It just happened. Just one of those things.

"I can't talk right now. I'll have to call you back."

I should just turn around. Walk away.

"Don't worry. Whichever way it goes, I'll be okay." She took a deep steadying breath. "No. I'm not worried."

The checker picked up one of her items. Scanned it. Set it back on the counter.

I froze as I recognized the pink box.

I turned around then, but it was too late.

My world tilted. I couldn't unsee what I had seen.

I felt a little sick to my stomach. This was not how it was supposed to go.

31

ISABELLA

I slipped my phone back into my pocket and paid for the pregnancy tests. Never hurt to have more than one.

Clutching the little paper bag in my hand, I turned and looked around. I needed to find Wesley. I'd had to leave him because I hadn't wanted to betray Jenna's confidence. Wesley didn't need to know that Jenna might be pregnant, certainly not before her own husband did.

Wesley was sitting on a little red stool at the old-fashioned soda fountain when I found him.

"Want a soda?" he asked, with a quick glance at me.

"Sure." I slid onto the barstool next to him. I didn't drink sodas as a rule, but this was one of those times when it wouldn't hurt to have a little treat.

"Make it two," he said to the young man, wearing a vintage hat and apron, behind the counter.

"Coming right up," he said.

"This is kinda cute," I said, referring to the soda fountain.

Wesley nodded, but kept his gaze straight ahead. He seemed fascinated by the whole soda fountain thing.

After the server set the two cups in front of us, Wesley took a bill from his money clip and slid it across the bar.

"Is everything okay?" Wesley asked me, after the server walked away, but he wasn't making eye contact.

"It will be," I said. "Everything okay with you?"

"It will be," he echoed.

I sipped the coke, enjoying the fresh bubbly carbonated water.

"Ready to walk?" he asked.

"Sure." He was acting strange. I wasn't one to say anything. I'd done the same thing yesterday.

We headed to the door, walking through the aisles of everything from candles to t-shirts to first aid bandages and kits.

"Do you feel better now that you've gotten the court thing behind you?" I asked.

"A bit relieved," I said. "It never should have happened."

Something in the way he said it sounded... regretful. It was the first time he'd talked about it this way. Maybe he was just tired.

"Sorry about yesterday," I said as he held the door for me and we stepped outside into the cold. I wasn't from here. Wasn't from a cold climate at all, but to me it felt like snow. It was possible that the weather forecasters had gotten it wrong.

It happened on occasion. When I got back to the house, I'd check my iPad weather apps and draw my own conclusion.

"About what?" he asked. There was something in his eyes. Something I hadn't seen before. Perplexed. Wary.

"I took off without a word. I'm sorry."

He looked away. Shook his head. "You have a lot to deal with right now," he said.

"Right." I put my head down against the gust of wind. That was an odd statement.

As we walked past a bookstore, a customer stepped out,

letting a classical Christmas song drift out to mingle with the one playing over the sidewalk speakers. It was a little discordant, but in a good way. I must be getting used to hearing sounds blended together that didn't really belong together.

Why would Wesley say that? Why would he think that I had a lot to deal with?

I put a hand on his arm to stop him and held it until his gaze met mine. His sparkling blue eyes were becoming familiar and dear to me.

Maybe now that his court date was over, he was disengaging himself from me.

There were so many reasons.

"Can we step inside the bookstore?" I asked. I had an idea. A private gift for Jenna from me to thank her for her hospitality and for lending me her dress and jacket.

"Of course," he said, moving to push the door open for me.

I planned on flying back to Houston later today, so I didn't have much time.

If I was going to say something about how I felt, then I had to do it now.

Hard to do when I didn't exactly know how I felt.

Besides, this was Whiskey Springs. Once I left, the spell could be broken. I was worrying about something that was nothing.

But for something that was nothing, it certainly did feel like everything.

32

WESLEY

The bookstore smelled like pines trees, leather, and vanilla. A large blue spruce Christmas tree standing in front of the window was decorated with hundreds of little miniature books, less an inch tall. They had little covers with recognizable titles and little blank pages inside. I didn't even know such a thing existed, but it was cool as shit. I was so impressed, that I took a picture to send to my mother and older sister who both loved to read.

It was also an excuse to let Isabella wander ahead of me.

My world felt like it had turned upside down.

Drawn to the warmth of the gas fireplace, I stood with one arm against the mantle, as my thoughts attempted to untangle themselves.

Isabella was one of the most compelling women I had ever met.

She was lovely with green eyes that reminded me of the story of the sirens who lured the sailors toward them, leading the sailors to their death across the rocks in the process.

Isabella may well be the death of me. I was drawn to her,

despite coming upon evidence that she could well be or perhaps should well be off limits.

I had heard her phone conversation telling someone that things would be okay either way. And that was *while* she had been in the process of buying a pregnancy test.

It explained what happened last night. Could explain her sudden need to be alone on a variety of levels.

Compelling evidence. That's what it was.

Compelling evidence that I should not fall in love with her.

But falling in love wasn't one of those things that a man could just decide to turn off like turning off a faucet.

In fact... as I learned more about her, whether it was something I liked or not, made me that much more interested in her. It was a paradoxical phenomenon.

I replayed her words.

Whichever way it goes, I'll be okay. No. I'm not worried.

It sounded like a conversation with a friend or a family member. Not so much a guy. Besides, she didn't wear a ring of any kind. No engagement ring.

It didn't give me a lot to go on, but the chivalrous nature she brought out in me from the beginning was still there. Maybe even stronger than ever.

I looked over my shoulder, caught a glimpse of her pulling a book off one of the shelves.

I wanted to tug her hair loose from the clip that help it at the back of her head and run my hands through it. I wanted to kiss those plump red lips.

Forcing my attention away from her, I looked back into the flames and pressed my fingers against my forehead.

My gut, which was all I had to go on, told me that Isabella was in trouble. Trouble defined as being pregnant without a father in the picture.

I knew it was the twenty-first century and all that. But I was embracing my newly discovered Neanderthal tendencies.

My heart had already decided that she was *the one* and I didn't see much point in fighting it. I'd always believed that my heart would know. And since my heart had never bothered to tell me this before, I figured it was all the more reason to trust it.

The problem was I wasn't sure her business was really any of my business.

Isabella had not told me that she was pregnant, so I wasn't supposed to know.

And if I wasn't supposed to know, then how was I was supposed to ask her about it.

It wasn't something to just come out and ask someone.

"I'm about to check out," Isabella said, coming up behind me. "Are you about ready to go or do you want to look around?"

"I'm ready," I said, following her to the checkout counter.

She laid the book on the counter and said something to me, but for the life of me, I didn't know what those words were.

The book was *What to Expect When You're Expecting.*

33

ISABELLA

*W*ispy white clouds gathered around the tall rugged mountain peaks, hiding them from view. Otherwise, the sky was clear. It was going to be a good day for flying.

Thinking about flying out this afternoon left me feeling a bit sick to my stomach. Not the flying part. It was the leaving part. Once I left here, I left Wesley behind.

Two chipmunks dashed up and sat up on their hind legs in front of us, begging for a bite of food. When they didn't get anything immediately, they skittered along to beg the next person. Unfortunately, no one had anything to give a couple of cute chipmunks.

Lunch at the Hungry Biscuit was apparently a popular activity in Whiskey Springs.

We had to take a pager and wait.

Since there was no room to wait inside, we waited outside.

There was one seat on a wooden bench next to an older couple. Wesley insisted that I sit while he stood next to me.

The air was cool, but the sun was warm on my skin.

I adjusted Wesley's scarf around my neck. I should probably

in all honesty give it back to him, but right now, since my coat was too light for the climate, I would probably freeze without it.

The older woman sitting next to me leaned close. "It's snowing in the high country," she said.

"The high country?" I asked. It seemed to me that Whiskey Springs was high in elevation, too. However, I suppose the mountains were high relative to here. It was all relative.

"You're not from here, are you Dear?"

"No," I said with a little smile.

"My husband and I have lived here for almost forty years. We met here and just stayed."

"Neither one of you are from here?" I asked.

"Oh no. We were both here on vacation for the summer with our parents. And as they say the rest is history."

"You must really like it here."

"We wouldn't want to live anywhere else. In fact." She lowered her voice as though it was a secret. "We went on a vacation once. Just once, mind you. We decided right then and there we didn't need to go anywhere else because we lived in the best place in the world."

"Wow." I couldn't imagine never going anywhere. Ever. I could hardly imagine not going anywhere for a week.

"What about your husband?" she asked. "He looks like he could be from here."

"No," I said. "He's not—" from here. He's not my husband. But I didn't know where he was from.

I only knew his last name because I had seen it on the flight manifest.

The older woman's pager went off before I had to answer any further.

"Take care of each other," she said before she stood up. "It's very important. Very important."

"We will," I said softly as Wesley sat down next to me.

"We will what?" he asked.

"Nothing," I said. I had slipped the drug store bag into the bag with the book I'd gotten for Jenna so I only had one bag to carry.

"Do you want me to hold that for you?" Wesley asked.

"No," I said with a little smile. "I'm okay."

"What book did you buy?" he asked.

It was an innocent question. One that anyone would be expected to ask if out of nothing more than politeness.

"It's just a book for a friend," I said, not wanting to tell him about Jenna.

He nodded slowly. "It's okay," he said. "You don't have to pretend."

34

WESLEY

*T*he snow-capped Rocky Mountains were hidden behind thick white clusters of clouds. Snow clouds.

Everyone knew that meant it was snowing up there and usually that meant that it would be snowing here down here in the little valley before long.

The forecasters insisted that there would be no snow for Christmas in Whiskey Springs, but they could be wrong. They had been wrong before.

The sun was warm in contrast to the cold wind sweeping down the mountains and across the bubbling river.

I hope the weather held for my flight tomorrow. I'd already texted Daniel and arranged the flight. So I would be in Pittsburgh tomorrow for Christmas Eve.

I could have flown out today, but since I hadn't known what would come off in court today, I didn't plan it.

Now I was glad I hadn't. It allowed me to spend time with Isabella that I wouldn't otherwise have had.

Right now, though, Isabella was looking at me as though I had lost my mind.

"It's not for me," she said. "It's for a friend."

"Okay," I said. I'd heard that one before. I just hadn't expected Isabella to use that excuse. She was a modern woman who could have a child by herself if she wanted to. Or maybe she had a boyfriend and just didn't want to tell me. That last one actually bothered me.

Our pager went off and we went inside the restaurant. It was loud inside. There was a layer of music somewhere beneath the voices.

The day before Christmas Eve and the town that was synonymous with Christmas was full of energy.

"I think it would be nice to spend Christmas here," I said, purposefully changing the subject, as we settled into our seats against the back wall.

"You aren't?"

"No. I changed my flight to tomorrow."

A server brought us glasses of cold water.

"I didn't know what you had decided," she said. "Why not today?"

"Needed to see what happened first."

"I'm leaving today," she said.

It felt like a kick in the gut. It didn't matter that I expected her to be leaving soon. Or maybe I didn't. Maybe since her brother lived here, I imagined her staying here, too.

"Back to Houston?"

"Yes."

"Daniel, too?"

"Yes. After he drops you off, he'll fly to Houston, too."

Everything felt... off.

Nothing was going as it should.

I shoved my menu aside and leaned forward.

"Look," I said. "I need to say something."

"Okay," she said, warily.

"I guess I should ask you something first." I was stalling now and I knew it. But somehow the words I wanted to say were getting stuck in my throat.

And now she was just looking blankly at me.

"Are you seeing anyone?" I asked.

"No."

"Good." I didn't think so. But now that I'd started, I couldn't turn away from the conversation. Sometimes the best way around a problem was to run right through the middle of it. "I can be a good father to your baby."

Her mouth dropped open.

"If you'll have me. With the pregnancy and the long-distance thing, we have to speed things up. But I'm okay with that. We don't have to wait."

"What are you talking about?"

She wasn't getting it. She didn't understand what I was trying to say. I ran a hand over my chin. What the hell?

I stood up, went to her side of the table, and dropped to one knee.

"Isabella Fleming," I said. "Will you marry me? I'll be a good husband and a good father to your baby."

35

ISABELLA

*T*he restaurant was crowded and noisy. Wesley and I had a table off to the side and no one was paying us any attention. A lot of people had family in for the holidays. Family they probably hadn't even seen in a year or maybe even more.

The place smelled like an appetizing mixture of fried foods and bread. Servers dashed here and there, all appearing to have someplace they needed to be.

Wesley had lost his mind.

He was kneeling at my feet. Right here in broad daylight.

I didn't care what anyone else thought about much of anything, but being the center of attention was not something I enjoyed. I was a private person who preferred to be left alone to do my own thing.

And right now, not only were we getting attention from tables around us, but Wesley had lost his mind.

"What are you doing?" I asked.

"I'm proposing."

"Stop it," I said. "You can't do this."

I honestly thought he was kidding around, but the hurt in his eyes was real.

When he was back in his seat, I scooted my chair next to his so I could talk to him without everybody in the world hearing.

"Wesley," I said. "I don't understand. You hardly know me."

"I know everything I need to know."

"Well I don't know anything about you."

That seemed to resonate with him.

"You're right," he said, looking into my eyes. "You don't."

Then he proceeded to tell me.

"I'm an engineer. I came up with an idea, got a patent, and sold the whole thing to a company. Since I don't have to go to a job every day, I'm an investor."

"My sister is an investor," I said, absently, but I don't think he heard me.

"I came to Whiskey Springs to check out a potential investment."

"What kind of invention?"

"A technological breakthrough that helps businesses with their WIFI."

"Oh," I said. I tried to wrap my head around how that might work. But it was an exercise in futility since I knew nothing about WIFI except that it worked.

"But that's not really the point," he said. "Or maybe it is. I can live anywhere. As an investor, I work from home."

I tried to make sense of what he was telling me.

I think he was telling me that he could marry me and take care of me.

And he thought I was pregnant.

The pregnancy test and the book. There was no way he could have seen the pregnancy test, but he saw the book. That was a lot of jumping to conclusions. Still…

"But why?"

"Because," he said and I realized I'd asked the question out loud.

It was a valid question. This wasn't the old days when a woman would be shunned from polite society for having a child out of wedlock.

Looking into my eyes, he swept a lock of hair off my cheek. "Because I like you."

Something in his sparkling blue eyes told me he really did like me. But... there was one problem with his thinking.

"I'm not pregnant," I said.

"How do you know? You haven't had time to—"

I put a hand on his wrist. "It's not for me," I said. There was only way I was going to get him to believe me. "It's for my sister-in-law."

"Jenna?"

"Please don't say anything. You can't know before Daniel."

He sat back in his chair and studied me.

"I guess you think I'm an idiot," he said, finally.

"No." I shook my head, feeling terrible. I didn't think he was an idiot. I thought he was a chivalrous and honorable man.

But he didn't have to marry me to save my reputation. I wasn't pregnant.

Nonetheless, his proposal had me feeling completely off-balance.

It had not only felt like a genuine proposal.

As I looked him. At the way he was smiling at me. At the way his eyes seemed to latch onto mine and see into my very soul.

It occurred to me that I had an overwhelming inclination to say yes.

36

WESLEY

*a*s far as bungling things up, this was on the top of my list. In fact, at the moment I couldn't think of anything that ranked higher.

I'd made assumptions because I wanted to. I'd looked for reasons.

And I had been wrong.

"I'm sorry," I said.

She put a hand over mine and smiled. "Don't be. It was an honest mistake."

She was being kind, of course. That was one of the many things about her I was drawn to.

So many women I'd met would have laughed or would have been offended.

"Which one do you think would be better here?" she asked, looking at the menu. "A grilled hamburger or the fried shrimp?"

I looked behind me at the table to our right. Then back to study the menu.

"The shrimp looks good," I said. "I'd go with the shrimp."

"That's what I'll have then," she said, closing her menu and setting it aside.

"I'll have the same."

And just as easily as I had bungled things up, she had smoothed them out.

"How long has it been since you lived in Pittsburgh?"

"I've lived there off and on since college."

"And now?"

"I have an apartment in Philadelphia."

"But you can live anywhere?"

The server came and took our orders. We both ordered the fried shrimp. She claimed it was one of her weaknesses. She knew all the best seafood places in Houston. Some good ones in Galveston, too.

"I can," I said, sitting back and lifting my glass of wine. "I can live anywhere. I've been considering buying a place—a house or a condo, but it just seemed like something a couple would do together, you know?"

She stopped, her glass halfway to her lips. "I do know," she said. "Have you decided where you might want to settle down?"

"Not really," I said. "I don't want to rush into buying something just because I can. I thought it best to get accustomed to not going to a day job first."

She grinned. "You sound like you've been talking to my grandmother. Or one of my aunts."

"Why is that?" I sat back as the server refilled our water glasses.

"We have a lot of psychologists in the family."

"Psychologists and pilots," I said. "A rather odd mix."

"Not really. It actually works well." She adjusted the napkin in her lap and sipped her wine. She hadn't moved her chair, so she was still sitting next to me instead of across from me. I liked it better this way.

"We have school teachers and bankers."

"Very traditional."

"I have a very traditional family," I said.

"That's where you get it."

"Where I get what?" I asked, my gaze dipping to her lips when she wasn't looking. I could never tire of looking at her.

"Your chivalrousness."

"I guess it is," I said. It was something I hadn't given much thought. I didn't tell her, but I hadn't noticed having much chivalrousness until I met her.

Sometimes all it took was finding the right person. Someone who brought out the parts of ourselves that we didn't know we had.

And this was the first time I halfway understood the expression about being someone's better half.

37

ISABELLA

I didn't know what I was going to do. Yet.

I did know that I wasn't ready to leave Whiskey Springs.

There were too many things left unresolved.

I'd purposely distracted him to give myself time to settle. To think.

The man had gotten on one knee and proposed to me, for God's sake.

That wasn't nothing.

I had been shocked. And, I had to admit, frightened.

Being in Whiskey Springs and getting a marriage proposal on my third night here?

My family would never ever let me live this down.

My siblings would say "I told you so" until they were blue in the face.

Maybe I wouldn't tell them.

But if I didn't tell them, then that meant not being with Wesley.

I liked Wesley. A lot.

And I wasn't ready to leave here because I wasn't ready to leave him.

It was a humbling realization.

After lunch, we walked along Main Street, taking our time in the crowded shops before we started the walk back to Jenna's parents' house.

Before I knew it, it was already getting dark. Somewhere along the way, it looked like I had decided to stay another night in Whiskey Springs.

Moonlight reflected off the twinkling, sparkling Christmas lights. We turned left down Elm Street and walked along the alley of blue spruce trees. Nature's Christmas trees. Decorated with pine cones and bird's nests. An old owl hooted in one of the branches as we walked along, slowly making our way down the street.

The trees smelled clean and tangy. The air here was so fresh it almost hurt to breathe it in.

Jenna's house was the largest on the street lined with old houses that looked like they had been here for hundreds of years.

Even though the house was old, it was clean and modern. They had added a wing onto the house at some point and built a glass room that brought the outdoors inside. If I was going to live anywhere besides the city, I would want to live somewhere like this. Somewhere beautiful and peaceful.

We walked right by Jenna's house to the end of the street, then stood next to a wooden rail fence, just soaking in the moonlight.

"It's beautiful here," I said, wrapping his scarf closer around me, then stuffing my hands back in my coat pockets, trying not to shiver. "The city is beautiful, too, but this is different."

"Agreed. It's hard to pick the one place to live."

I turned and looked at him, his eyes bright in the moonlight.

"That's the thing," I said with a little smile. "You don't have to pick just one place to live. You can have a house in the city and a house... here."

"You have a different perspective from most people."

I shrugged. "I guess it comes from being a pilot. My grandparents used to have a cabin up here in the mountains, but I think they finally decided to sell it."

He leaned back, his elbows on the fence. "I could definitely live here."

"They say there's a magic here," I said, shivering now.

"I've heard that." He turned to face me. "You're freezing."

Before I had time to realize what he was doing, he pulled me close and wrapped his arms around me. His coat was open enough that I rested my cheek against his shirt. As I soaked in his warmth, I felt his heart beating.

I sighed.

It felt so very right to be here with him. Right now. At this moment.

"Isabella," he said, softly.

"Hmm?" I did not want to move. Ever.

"Look." He gently nudged me back and I reluctantly opened my eyes.

"What?"

"It's snowing."

It was snowing. Tomorrow was Christmas Eve and the magic of Whiskey Springs was all around us. I laughed when a big, fluffy flake landed on my eyelashes.

Smiling, I looked up at Wesley.

He pressed his lips lightly on one cheek.

Then he kissed me.

I'd resisted the magic of Whiskey Springs, but Wesley pulled me under. I was swept away by the undertow and I knew I was lost.

My last logical thought came and went like a wispy snow cloud.

Tomorrow. Tomorrow I needed to leave Whiskey Springs.

If not, I'd probably find myself at the altar.

38

WESLEY

*T*he magic of Whiskey Springs.

As an engineer, I shouldn't believe in such an illogical phenomenon.

But that would be like someone saying they didn't believe in love in first sight.

I believed in both.

There were some things a man probably had to experience to believe in. This was probably one of them.

"You're freezing," I said. "I need to get you inside."

Hand in hand, Isabella and I walked back to Jenna's house.

"I think you missed your flight," I said.

Isabella laughed. "I think you're right. I did."

"Maybe you can catch one out tomorrow."

"I think it's likely." She didn't look up as she said the words.

"You can hitch a ride with me," I said, squeezing her hand.

"Yeah," she said. "I can do that."

I ignored the lack of conviction in her voice. It was cold and it was snowing.

I would get her inside, then tomorrow, we would have the

morning and the long flight to Pittsburgh to figure out our next step.

I knew what I wanted our next step to be.

I'd known the moment I'd seen her. I just hadn't realized it.

And now that I had kissed her, even the logical part of my brain agreed wholeheartedly and was working on how to make a legitimate proposal. One that was planned out and didn't send Isabella into shock.

Surprise was okay, but not shock.

But now that I had found her, I didn't want to wait. I didn't want to be apart from her. Not even for a minute.

It was illogical. Unexpected. And wonderful.

When we reached the door, she punched a code into the door's keypad and the lock slid open.

With one hand on the doorknob, she turned and looked up at me.

I pulled her into my arms and sank her into a deep kiss.

She sighed and leaned against me, letting go of the doorknob, and wrapping her arms around me.

She was perfect. She fit perfectly against me. Her lips were sweet and her kiss matched mine.

But it was time to let her go before I couldn't. Before evening turned into morning and my arms were still wrapped around her.

"I'll see you in the morning," I whispered.

Pushing away, she looked at me with sleepy eyes. Squeezing my hands, she leaned forward and kissed me on the cheek.

"Goodnight," she said, then opened the door and slipped inside.

"Goodnight," I said to the closed door.

I stood and waited until I heard the door lock click into place. Then I turned and looked out over the valley toward the mountain peaks.

The mountains were just a faint outline in the moonlight. If

I didn't know they were there, I don't think I would have noticed them.

Inhaling deeply, I breathed in the intoxicating scent of the blue spruce trees scattered about the lawn and lining the street.

Isabella had said I could live here.

It was funny because it hadn't occurred to me.

I could go anywhere and live anywhere. I only stayed in Philadelphia because that was where I had last worked.

I thought of it as home. Oddly enough it had somehow become more home than Pittsburg where I had grown up.

The thought that I could live anywhere I wanted to was a freeing sensation. I knew it, of course, logically, but I hadn't actually added it into my belief system. Born and bred in Pennsylvania, that was where I lived. Where I thought I would always live. It wasn't even something I consciously ever thought about and now I felt a little bit silly.

As I walked down the front porch stairs, I smiled to myself.

Isabella was so very right.

We could live mainly in Houston near her family. I'd never spent any time in Houston, but I was sure it was a perfectly fine city.

She also had a brother who lived here in Whiskey Springs. We could have a house here, maybe a cabin, but a nice one. Big enough to accommodate the children.

I was getting ahead of myself.

But I knew where I wanted to go.

I just needed to figure out how to get there.

39

ISABELLA

I woke early. Four a.m. The gentle chiming of my phone's alarm an unwelcome reminder of what I had to do. It was four in the morning here, but already five o'clock in Houston.

It was Christmas Eve, but for the first time in my life, I didn't feel the magic that had always come along with my favorite time of the year.

Instead, I felt a deep wounding sadness that haunted me down to the core.

After a quick hot shower, I carefully hung Jenna's dress and jacket in the closet. Put on my jeans and sweatshirt that I had washed yesterday morning.

I packed everything—not much at all—into my overnight bag.

Finding a piece of stationary in the writing desk drawer, I sat down and wrote Jenna a little note. I folded it, wrote her name on the outside, and left it on the desk, along with the pregnancy book and the pregnancy test.

I'd send her a text later in the morning with an explanation.

I put on my coat, then picked up the red scarf that belonged to Wesley. Considered.

If I left the scarf here, there was no guarantee that he would get it.

Sitting in the armchair, I carefully folded it, then held it up and breathed in the rich clean scent that reminded me of Wesley.

I allowed myself a moment to replay his kisses in my head.

Then I straightened and, unfolding the scarf, I wrapped it around my neck and looped it in front. I should have given it back to him last night, but I hadn't been thinking. I'd barely been able to keep a single thought other than him in my head.

I would just keep it. A scarf wasn't something a guy would be overly attached to. He probably wouldn't even notice that I still had it.

I stood up and surveyed the room. Everything was in order. It would be so easy to stay. So easy to catch the flight with my brother to Houston. Drop Wesley off in Philadelphia then be home for Christmas Eve.

But that wasn't what I had to do. I wasn't ready for that.

Slipping out the door, I quietly walked down the hallway toward the stairs. So far so good. I didn't have an explanation ready, so it was best to slip out undetected.

As I made my way down the stairs, I called myself an idiot. Wesley was *the one*. But I had promised myself to not get caught up in the magic of Whiskey Springs.

Since I'd met him here and had fallen in love with him here, I couldn't know if it was real. I would always wonder if it was actually just the magic spell that had befallen my siblings.

I wanted to know that it was real before I took my walk down the altar.

I made it all the way to the kitchen without incident. Then I made a mistake. I ducked into the kitchen to grab a bottle of water from the refrigerator.

"Where are you going?"

I jumped and turned around. Daniel, bathed in the soft glow of a lamp, was sitting at the breakfast table reading a newspaper.

A newspaper?

Only in Whiskey Springs.

My pulse still pounding dangerously, I walked over so that I could look him in the eye.

"I'm going home," I said, feeling a bit like the little sister that I was. It couldn't be helped. Once a little sister, always a little sister.

Daniel pushed the newspaper aside and pushed out a chair with his foot.

"Sit," he said.

I made a face, but I sat down anyway, dropping my tote bag on the floor beside me.

"Why?" he asked.

"It's Christmas Eve and I have things to do."

Daniel narrowed his eyes at me. "No," he said. "That's not it."

I said nothing. Sometimes it was best to stay quiet.

"No," he said again. "You're running away."

"I am not," I said reflexively, but he was right and we both knew it.

"Did you tell him?" he asked.

I shook my head and looked away, wrapping my hands in Wesley's scarf.

"You should at least tell him."

"I know that," I said, looking back at him. He was making this much harder. I only had so much resolve. And he was chipping at it.

"It's not a curse, you know."

"What's not a curse?"

"Falling in love."

"It's Whiskey Springs," I said as though that explained everything. And for me it did.

Daniel smiled and picked up his coffee cup.

"You can't seriously think that it matters." He sat his cup down and leaned forward, searching my face. "But you do. You do think it matters. Because you've fallen in love with him."

"You don't know," I said.

"Of course I do," he said, leaning back again in his chair. "I'm your older brother. I know everything."

I let out a sigh. I hated that he was right and that he knew it. But I was a little bit relieved. Daniel could stop me from doing what I knew in my heart was a mistake.

"How are you getting to Denver?" he asked.

Startled, I looked at him. "I have a car coming at five."

"Then you'd better get out there," he said. "It's time."

"Right," I said. I hesitated, but he just picked up his newspaper and started reading again.

I picked up my tote bag as I stood up and left the kitchen.

I wasn't sure, but I think I heard him say. "You aren't making this easy on the poor guy."

All I knew was that Daniel wasn't going to stop me.

And I had secretly hoped that he would.

40

WESLEY

*T*he morning had gone by in a whirlwind. Not at all what I had expected.

Daniel had called, telling me that we needed to leave early to get ahead of a storm in Pittsburgh.

I hadn't talked to my mother in a couple of days and my weather app wasn't giving me much information about a storm, but I trusted Daniel's judgement. Stopped at the coffee shop on my way to the Whiskey Springs airport to grab a coffee and a muffin.

The sun was barely up, casting a wash of gold through the clouds as it splashed over the tops of the snow-capped mountains. It tumbled over the mountains into the valley settling softly over Main Street. And with the soft glow of the just-risen sun, came a flurry of early-morning activity.

Due to that early morning rush of activity in town, I had to wait in line for my coffee. Keeping an eye on my watch, I waited impatiently in line. I kept reminding myself that the plane didn't leave without me.

It was a rather odd feeling. And along with it I felt a sense of pride that my girlfriend was a pilot.

My girlfriend...

My thoughts tripped over the possibility of calling Isabella my girlfriend. That was one of the things she and I needed to talk about.

One of the many things.

By the time my coffee was ready, my car was waiting just outside.

Another interesting thing. The airport brought jobs a lot of people wouldn't think about. Like drivers to the airport and back. Pretty soon they would need a parking lot out there. They could charge for that, too.

The airport was a brilliant move on Noah Worthington's part. One of the main reasons I had come to check out the possibility of investment property here. I had pretty much decided to do it, but there were some details to work out.

The Phenom sat in the middle of the tarmac. The steps down and waiting. The door opened invitingly.

By the time I had my suitcase waiting next to the airplane, Daniel came to the door at the top of the stairs. He was wearing his pilot's uniform and cap.

"Morning," he said. "Ready to come aboard?"

"I'm ready." I tried to look past him, hoping to catch sight of Isabella. "Pretty day," I said as he loaded my suitcase.

"They're looking for snow," he said.

"Here?" I followed him up the stairs into the airplane. The smell reminded me of a new car.

"Maybe," he said. "Sit anywhere you like."

All six seats were empty. Daniel closed the door and secured everything. As he went toward the cockpit, I looked for Isabella, but when Daniel sat down and put on his headphones, he was the only pilot.

"Mind if sit here for a while?" I asked, indicating the empty copilot's seat.

"Go head," he said. "Buckle up."

I did as he said.

Maybe Isabella was running late.

But even as the thought came to mind, I realized we were moving.

Enough with all this.

"Where's Isabella?" I asked.

Daniel looked over, his expression blank, then focused his attention back on the computer screens.

"She drove in to Denver to take a direct flight to Houston."

That explained why she wasn't here. But it didn't explain the reason.

"Anything wrong?" I asked, over the sound of the engine.

"I don't think so," he said.

Then we were in the air.

Daniel held up a headset for me to put on. Now I could hear his voice clearly through the headset.

"We have about fifteen minutes before I have to lock in our final route."

"Okay," I said.

"But first I need to know something."

Daniel was wearing dark shades and I couldn't see his eyes. Something was up. Something that could be a little intimidating if I let it. I refused to do so.

"What are your intentions toward my sister?"

41

ISABELLA

*a*fter arriving at the Denver airport and checking in, I stood in line to board the plane.

I'd almost forgotten what a hassle it was to fly commercial. It made me appreciate flying private all the more. As I took off my shoes and had my tote bag searched by a stranger, I had another reason to regret my decision to not fly with Wesley and Daniel on the Phenom.

My seat was 27B, so I was one of the first to board the jet. I sat watching people as they boarded the plane. It was Christmas Eve, so most people looked relatively happy.

Someday everyone would have their own private airplane and people wouldn't have to travel packed into air buses like this.

But that was a long long way away. And just like with buses on the ground, there would be people who couldn't afford their own plane or afford to run it.

And then they would have to make them a whole lot easier to learn how to fly than they were now.

I took out my phone and toyed with it. I didn't feel like texting anyone. I just wanted to sit here and hope that the

Whiskey Springs spell lessened as I got further away. So far it wasn't happening.

The flight attendant said something over the speaker. I ignored it and watched the crew as they slid suitcase after suitcase from the car tossing them to the underside of the airplane.

"Isabella Fleming." The flight attendant said my name as she stood next to my seat.

"Yes," I said. I didn't know of anything I had done wrong. A quick glance around told me that no one else seem concerned about anything. So that meant this was just about me.

"Will you come with me?" she asked.

"Why?"

"Get your bag," she said, not answering me.

My nerves on edge, I pulled my overnight bag from the overhead storage compartment.

The flight attendant was already several feet away, obviously expecting me to follow her.

Was I actually being escorted from the airplane?

Why? I hadn't said anything to anyone. I hadn't caused any trouble.

If someone in my family needed me, they would contact me by phone. I glanced at the cell phone in my hand. No messages. No calls.

Maybe there was a problem with my paperwork.

Baffled, I followed her down the aisle toward the door.

I had no choice and I knew it.

"What did I do wrong?" I asked when I caught up with her at the door.

"You didn't do anything wrong, Dear," she said.

"Then what?"

"You can come right back," she said, pushing the door open. "If you want to."

She nodded her head and I stepped through the door. As I

walked down the hallway back to the gate, I wracked my brain for any reason that I was being asked to leave the airplane. Since I wasn't being escorted, it must not be too bad.

I'd never been in trouble.

She said I could come back. What did that mean?

I gave up on trying to figure it all out by the time I reached the gate. There was a line at the coffee kiosk and a few people walking along the concourse, but no one at my gate.

If I didn't get back to the airplane, I was going to miss my flight. Maybe it was some kind of joke. Maybe an experiment.

Okay. The joke was on me. I would just go back to the airplane.

I turned around and nearly bumped right into Wesley Bennett.

"Hi," he said.

"Hi. What—"

"You missed your flight," he said.

I tried to smile, but I didn't know if I was successful or not. My heart was racing and I felt a little short of breath.

"I 'um…"

He brought a rose from behind his back and held it out to me.

As I took it in my hands, my eyes misted over with unshed tears and I bit my lower lip to keep it from trembling.

"I don't understand."

"I made an assumption and bungled everything up." He swept a finger over my lips. "I was hoping you would forgive me."

"But… how are you here?"

"My pilot gave me the option of taking a detour."

I smiled then, some of the tension draining away. Daniel. Daniel would have known where to find me. He would have been able to get here to intercept my flight if he wanted to.

And since Wesley was here, that meant he wanted to.

"Down to the wire," I said.

"You're not kidding."

"But why?"

He took my tote bag, set it on the floor, and pulled me into a hug.

Resting my cheek against his chest, I realized just how happy I was to have him here. Just how relieved that I hadn't been able to carry out my plan to run away from him.

"Maybe you'll give me a second chance," he said. "And this time I'll court you properly."

"Okay," I said. But I wasn't so sure that people ever really started over. Second chances, yes, but we had a base now that couldn't be erased.

I hadn't been ready to fall in love.

But now, standing here with Wesley, I remembered my own words to Jenna.

Everything will come together. No one is ever ready when it happens, but life shifts and accommodates.

Perhaps it was my turn to have an open mind. To let go of my preconceptions of how things should go.

Pulling back, both of my hands clasped in his, I looked into his sparkling blue eyes.

It was Christmas Eve.

And this Christmas Eve suddenly shimmered with magic.

The magic of Whiskey Springs or not, I had just been given the best gift of a lifetime.

"Is that a yes?" he asked.

I nodded. "Yes." I pressed a hand against his cheek, rough with a light stubble.

"Merry Christmas, love," he said and then his lips were on mine with a kiss.

It was a wonderful, magical Christmas Eve and I had been rescued by my knight in shining armor.

Keep Reading for a preview of FINDING NATALIE...

NOTE FROM THE AUTHOR

Whiskey Springs. A little western town with a sparkle of magic.

If you finished reading An Old Fashioned Christmas, you may have read all five of my Whiskey Springs Christmas books. So in case you missed the introduction, I'd like to tell you a little about Whiskey Springs.

Whiskey Springs is a fictional town located somewhere west of Denver, deep in the Rocky Mountains. Its exact location has never been mapped. It is believed, however, to be somewhere near the Rocky Mountain National Park.

The magic element of Whiskey Springs began in the late 1800s when the town was filled only with men who'd left behind the war-ravaged states and traveled west to an unknown, but better place.

These men built the town around one establishment—the Whiskey Springs saloon—where whiskey was known to flow freely. Before long the area had a stable for horses, a General Store, and a little restaurant.

Many men found wives here. Some of them were reunited from another time and place. Some were new and unexpected love at first sight romances.

The men who settled in this little fictional town were determined and steadfast. They took care of their own, no matter the cost.

My historical romance series explores the early days of this wild western town—as Whiskey Springs was being settled. These are bold stories of love and adventure in the untamed west.

While the western series explores the beginning of the town, the contemporary Christmas series shows the little town all grown up.

In the modern version of the town, Whiskey Springs is synonymous with Christmas. After all, there is no more magical time than Christmas.

Taking into account its mystic nature, it comes as no surprise that Whiskey Springs is also featured in some of my time travel romances starting with Dragon's Blood. Five siblings. Five soulmates who travel to the past to be with them. Defying all odds, crossing the boundaries of time itself, these people find their true place in time.

Each couple, whether past, present, or through time, has their own journey to happily ever after.

As you visit each time period you will find common elements, perhaps most importantly, the Whiskey Springs Saloon.

The saloon is still there, along with a coffee shop, Smedley's Ice Cream shop, and a restaurant named the Hungry Biscuit. One never goes hungry or thirsty in Whiskey Springs.

I like to think that the romance of Whiskey Springs originated with the Whiskey Springs saloon. The saloon, also a hotel, and home to many over the years, perhaps holds one of the many keys that can bring couples together.

It has been there for centuries and, although the magic is subtle, and rarely noticed by most, I think it will continue to draw people together, at least those who need a little shove toward finding their one true love.

Whiskey Springs. Where the clean, fresh air carries the fragrance of blue spruce trees, snow clouds cluster around the rugged mountain peaks, and the air itself is laced with romance and happily ever after.

Stop by. Explore the past or the present, or if you're feeling a little more adventurous, jump into one of the time travels.

But most of all, take a moment to reflect on the spell of true love and the way it weaves its way through our lives and in the end holds everything together.

Yours truly,

Kathryn Kaleigh

February 2023

FINDING NATALIE

They made a promise in another place and time...

Natalie Worthington. A young lady who sacrifices everything to care for her family, but nearly loses her own life in the process.

When her father unexpectedly returns home from the Civil War, Natalie risks her life to save him. After the war, with nothing left and nowhere to go, they travel west. But danger lurks at every turn. Can she protect not only her loved ones, but also herself?

Alexander Avery. A loyal friend who got more than he bargained for. Unable to find the woman he loves, he travels west. To make a new life for himself.

Can Natalie and Alexander fulfill a promise made long ago in a place far, far away and find their forever?

A sweet, wholesome frontier western romance with a happily ever after. Read Finding Natalie to see how Whiskey Springs began.

PREVIEW FINDING NATALIE

1864

*T*here was something magical about a snowy morning.

The world was quiet and peaceful.

Absolutely no sounds whatsoever. Like a soft blanket insulating the earth.

Quiet except for Biscuit's soft snoring. The dog was curled up on the foot of her bed, keeping her feet warm.

Biscuit was a big gangly black dog. He'd shown up on their doorstep about a year ago, just a puppy then. He still acted like a puppy, but was in a grown dog's body.

Natalie Worthington rolled over and looked out the window. The snow was still coming down like heavy rain.

Pulling the blankets up beneath her chin, she considered the possibility of staying in bed all day.

Less than four long years ago, she could have done it. That

was before her father had left for the war and her mother was still alive.

But now her nine-year-old brother, Declan, was asleep down the hall and it was her responsibility to make sure he was fed and did his chores.

Finding enough food for him to eat was a full-time job.

The two of them worked from sunup to sundown just trying to survive.

Declan had gotten good at chopping firewood and liked to be outside.

Even today with the snow coming down, he'd see going outside to gather firewood as a grand adventure.

Unfortunately, that left Natalie with a world of other things to do. Like making sure Declan had dry clothes.

And lots of food to eat.

The Yankees had been through here about six months ago.

No matter what Doc said, Natalie believed that having the Yankees sitting on her settee was what sent her mother to her grave.

The Yankees had been cordial enough and had been respectful enough — contrary to the stories she'd heard about the havoc the enemy sometimes wreaked. Unfortunately, war was still war.

But without the war and their dreaded blue uniforms, the captain and his men would have been welcome guests in their home.

They had taken over the downstairs part of the house, leaving Natalie, her brother, and her mother privacy in the upstairs part.

It hadn't done them much good though. The kitchen was a separate building from the house. A feature common to all southern houses of any size.

So Natalie and her little family had to go downstairs and out the back door to get to the kitchen. That meant that every time her mother walked past the parlor, she saw the enemy lounging on her good furniture.

After the first day of making the trip to the kitchen outside, they'd started hoarding food upstairs to avoid walking past the soldiers three times a day.

The Yankees had been in the house for four days.

Mother had taken sick the same day the Yankees had marched away.

Natalie would have gone into town for the doctor, but the soldiers took the one horse they had left.

War was war.

So she'd sent Declan to the neighbor's house and asked them to send for the doctor.

When the doctor got there two days later, it was too late.

The doctor said it was her heart.

That it wasn't something sudden.

It didn't matter what the doc said, Natalie would go to her own grave knowing it was having Yankees in the house that had killed her. Her mother hadn't been able to see past the blue uniform.

And the knowledge that her husband was out there somewhere, most likely fighting against men wearing the same color uniform.

Natalie tossed the blankets aside and put her feet on the cold floor.

Shivering, she found her slippers, slipped them on, and wrapped her heavy cloak around her.

She needed to go out to the kitchen and get the fire going for breakfast.

Most days she went by herself out to the kitchen and made breakfast.

But today, she was reluctant to leave without Declan.

She tiptoed down the wide hallway and peeked into her brother's room.

"Declan?"

One thing she'd learned. Nine-year-old boys could sleep like the dead.

She went over and shook her brother.

He sat up, his eyes wide. "What's wrong?"

"Nothing," she said quickly. "It's snowing. We need to get to the kitchen before we get snowed in here."

He wiped at his eyes and nodded.

Natalie went back to her own room to get dressed.

She splashed cold water on her face and immediately regretted it as she shivered from the cold water.

She put on her warmest wool dress, thick socks, and her boots. Then put her cloak back on.

She ran a brush through her hair and was ready for the day. Or at least as ready as she was going to be.

She met her brother in the hall. He, too, was wearing warm clothes and a cloak.

"We'll come back later today and get all our blankets," she said. "We need to start sleeping in the kitchen. It'll be easier to keep warm."

"All right," Declan said.

She knew Declan didn't care one way or the other.

As long as he had plenty to eat and a warm place to sleep at night, not much else mattered.

He had a sadness about him now that was unnatural on a nine-year-old boy.

But it couldn't be helped.

It was the world they lived in.

Natalie focused on just surviving.

They'd survived a Yankee invasion and the loss of their parents. Now they needed to survive the first winter on their own.

They could do it.

Natalie just had to remember everything their parents had done and everything they'd been taught.

Natalie and Declan had done some fast growing up in these four years since the war started and even more since losing their mother.

But she was determined to keep the two of them alive.

Whatever it took.

And today it took moving them out of the big house into the kitchen. Fortunately, the kitchen was as big as many people's cabins, so it would be so much easier to stay warm in there.

The kitchen had actually become an integral part of their lives. A big stone fireplace for cooking and heating water. They even kept the cast iron bathtub in there so they didn't have to haul hot water to the house.

Walking together, Biscuit following along at their heels, they made their way down the hallway, down the stairs, and looked at each other before going outside.

"Ready?" she asked.

"No," Declan said.

But he opened the door anyway.

And they stepped outside into the snowstorm.

It was times like this that Natalie wished her grandfather had built a small cabin for them to live in instead of a grand manor house.

In a cabin, the kitchen would have been inside the house. A much simpler life than tramping through a snow storm… or a rain storm just to get something to eat.

Natalie put her head down as they walked the hundred yards or so to the kitchen.

Biscuit darted around them in his gangly way, stirring up even more clouds of snow.

About halfway to the kitchen, Natalie stopped and, shading her eyes, peered through the snow.

She smelled wood smoke.

There was already smoke coming from the kitchen's chimney.

She thought back to last night. Had they accidentally left enough wood in the fireplace that had kept burning all night?

No. Not possible. She was very careful about extinguishing the fire before they left the kitchen at night. They couldn't afford to have the kitchen burn down.

"There's somebody in the kitchen," Declan said.

"Wait." Natalie put a hand on his shoulder to hold him back.

It could be Yankees. Or worse. It could be southern renegades.

It would be just the worst luck to survive a Yankee invasion only for them to be taken down by renegades.

Renegades were far more dangerous than soldiers. Soldiers had a code.

Renegades had no code. No honor.

Biscuit took off, running toward the kitchen door. Natalie had to hold Declan back with both hands to keep him from going after the dog.

Even though Biscuit sometimes slept on her bed, Biscuit followed Declan around all day. As far as either of them were concerned, Biscuit was Declan's dog.

"We'll look in the window," she said.

They made their way through the falling snow to the window on this side of the kitchen.

Natalie held a finger up to her lips as they reached the window.

They peered in through the window, but the glass was fogged over.

All Natalie could see was a blazing fire in the fireplace.

She blinked away the snowflakes on her eyelashes and squinted to look closer.

There was a man sitting in front of the fireplace, just off to one side.

He was a Confederate soldier. Natalie could tell immediately by how tattered he looked.

It wasn't just his tattered uniform that she recognized. She recognized the hunched shoulders and defeated stance even from here.

But he wasn't close enough for her to recognize his features.

"We have to go back to the house," she said.

Declan nodded. "Are we gonna shoot him?"

"Are we gonna…" She started to tell him to watch his mouth. Then thought better about it. It was a valid question.

"I don't know yet," she said. "I have to figure it out."

They walked back through the snow and went back inside the house.

"I'll get the gun," Declan said, dashing upstairs.

It was bad when a nine-year-old knew where the guns were.

And even worse that he knew how to shoot. They'd both spent some time outside practicing. But that was so they could hunt for food. At least that's what she told him.

Something was nagging at the back of her mind.

Something other than the knowledge that they couldn't just shoot the man. Maybe he was just passing through. Maybe heading home.

And needed someplace warm to rest. Someplace out of the snow.

A minute later, Declan came running back down the stairs with the gun.

"Declan, don't run with the gun."

"Sorry," he said, slowing down a little bit.

She took the gun from him. "We aren't going to shoot him."

"Because he's a southerner?"

"Because it's wrong to go around shooting people," she said.

Even Declan could tell the man was a southerner.

Declan looked up at her with big round eyes. "Natalie?"

"What is it?" she asked.

They were standing just inside the front door. What used to be a grand foyer with paintings and a grandfather clock.

But now was just an entranceway. The paintings and clock had been taken by the Yankees. What was left, she and Declan had used for firewood.

"I'm hungry," Declan said.

They had no food here in the main house. The only way to get something for them to eat was to go into the kitchen.

"Dang it," Natalie leaned against the wall. There was no easy answer.

"Dang it," Declan echoed.

Natalie covered her face to hide a smile.

It was times like this that reminded her that he was still just a child.

It was so easy to forget.

Natalie was seventeen. Eight years older than Declan. She should be thinking about getting married about now.

Not contemplating whether or not they were going to have to shoot a man who'd camped out in their kitchen.

Shoot a man or starve.

Surely there was another option.

They'd even stopped keeping firewood in the house.

So if they didn't get to the kitchen, they would not only starve to death, they'd freeze to death.

She had to do something.

There had to be another answer.

"You stay here," she said. "I'll go ask him to leave."

She checked the gun. To make sure it was loaded, even though she knew it was.

"No," Declan said. "You can't go without me." He was the grown up Declan now.

"You hang back then," she said. "Did you bring the pistol?"

"I'll go get it," he said, then darted back up the stairs to get the pistol.

Natalie stood tall and steeled herself. She had to do it. She had to confront the man. Ask him to leave. He could sleep in the stables if he needed a place to stay.

Declan made it back with the other gun and they set off again. Into the cold, blinding snow.

"Remember," Natalie said. "You hang back in case I need help. We have to believe he's a peaceful man until we learn otherwise."

Declan grinned through chattering teeth. "Innocent until proven guilty," he said.

"Exactly."

Declan stopped at the edge of the kitchen building.

Natalie straightened her shoulders and moved forward.

She could do this.

If not for herself, for Declan.

She lifted up the rifle and put her hand on the doorknob.

Just get this over with.

She opened the door slowly.

The man turned and looked at her.

He had a heavy beard. And like she'd noticed before, his clothes and demeanor were tattered. Tired.

She held the gun up, pointing it at his chest. The gun was heavy. And she knew she couldn't hold it like this very long.

She had to be quick.

"Sir," she said. "I must ask you to leave my home." She shifted her hold on the gun. "You're welcome to stay in our barn if you need a place to weather the storm."

The man straightened, but didn't stand. Looked right at her and squinted.

"Natalie," he said. He spoke her name softly. Almost reverently. Not a question. Not surprised.

Recognition skittered along Natalie's spine.

She knew this man.

He was her father.

Keep Reading FINDING NATALIE...

Kathryn Kaleigh writes sweet contemporary romance, time travel romance, and historical romance.

kathrynkaleigh.com